RIGHT GUY, WRONG WORD

JEWEL E. ANN

RIGHT GUY, WRONG WORD

JEWEL E. ANN

This book is a work of fiction. Any resemblances to actual persons, living or dead, events, or locales are purely coincidental.

Cover Designer: Emily Wittig

Formatting: Jenn Beach

AUTHOR'S NOTE

This story was originally published as a short story, *The Last Person*. It has been revised and expanded into a full-length novel.

To every person who has felt the soul of a book

CHAPTER ONE

To EVERYONE who doesn't believe in global warming, suck it! That smell? It's my skin burning. I bet it resembles a hog roast. Someone, please give me a quarter turn.

Des Moines, Iowa, is not immune to summer heat. Still, ninety-seven degrees on the second day of June feels like Satan has come for Midwesterners first—surprising since everyone knows Las Vegas should be his priority.

I swipe my arm across my sweaty forehead and guide my bicycle into the entry of my apartment building in East Village—a quaint neighborhood of bars, shops, and modern-industrial apartments nestled between the capitol and downtown.

"Dear god ... yes." I stop and close my eyes, letting the cool air extinguish my skin. "Yes ... yes ... yes ..." I moan, stretching the neck of my drenched, fitted tee to wipe more sweat from my face. When I open my eyes, a new face greets me. The corner of his mouth bends in amusement, and I shoot him a tight smile. "It's sweltering outside."

He scratches the back of his neck before running his hand through his dark hair. "Something's definitely hot." Then he sets his bike next to him, slipping on bike gloves.

With a nervous laugh, I avert my gaze and focus on lifting my bike onto the rack. "Well, if you don't have to go out there, I wouldn't. I think I just burned three layers of skin on my neck."

"It's okay. I like the heat." He takes my bike from me, lifting it onto the rack.

"Thanks, but I could have done it. I do it every day."

He shrugs. "My mom says chivalry's dead. It's my life's mission to prove her wrong."

"Courageous, courteous, and a man of honor? Well, that would make you rare. I fear I have to agree with your mom." I wrinkle my nose and grin.

He curls his lips between his teeth and hums. "A shame."

"It really is."

"Anna." My roommate Freya interrupts my runaway thoughts over finding the last true gentleman on earth—right here in the middle of Iowa. "It's your month. I'll provide the wine, of course." She pins a flyer to the community board.

The new guy walks his bike to the board. "Book club, huh?"

"Yes. Eric, you should come ... if you like to read. We're starting a new book, and it's Anna's pick. There are twelve of us. We'll meet on the roof if it's not raining and in the lounge if the weather's bad. You'd be the fourth guy."

"Anna ..." he turns toward me.

"Oh ... did you just meet?" Freya flips her red, humidity-beaten hair over her shoulder and digs her car keys out of her pocket.

"Sort of." Eric smiles. It's a magnificent smile. It fits his last-of-the-good-men personality.

I'm not sure why I'm smiling. Sweat-crusted hair clings to my face like a hairy octopus attacked me. And that odor? Yeah, that's me.

"Anna, this is Eric Steinmann. He moved into Trent's old apartment two days ago. You were mysteriously missing that day." She gives me an accusatory smirk.

I spent the night and the following day with Carson, a local food blogger and a YouTube sensation. He adopted a service dog that lost one of his legs (after saving his previous owner when someone ran a red light), and his channel blew up with followers.

Everyone loves Gilbert, the three-legged yellow lab.

We're not a thing, but we enjoy doing *things* when neither of us is in a relationship, which is now.

Fun.

Easy.

Noncommittal.

"Anna is my roommate, and she works at the bouldering gym."

"That's cool." Eric bobs his head several times.

"Eric is opening a T-shirt shop next to your favorite coffee shop."

"Cool." I return the same sentiment.

"Yes. You're both super cool." Freya rolls her eyes and saunters out the door.

"Well ... I guess I'll see you around," I say with a tight-lipped smile.

"What book?"

"Huh?" I stop my advance toward the stairs and glance over my shoulder.

"What book did you pick for our book club?"

"*The Last Person* by B. Ashton."

"Huh ... never heard of it." He narrows his eyes.

"It's a murder mystery. A psychological thriller with a splash of romance."

"Interesting. I'll have to download it."

He's joining the book club. That's ... great. I think.

CHAPTER TWO

Book Club Night One

"Are you nervous?" Freya asks as she opens bottles of wine that she gets for a discount because she works at a local winery.

I finish arranging the trays of finger foods before our book club members make their way to the rooftop. "Nervous?" I clarify in a shaky voice.

"Your book choice. If people don't like it, you'll feel judged. Don't you remember when I picked that paranormal romance? I swear Ashlee and Devin still cringe when they see me."

"It was the period scene." I laugh.

"He could have killed her, but he loved her. I wish I could find a man as accepting of my monthly cycles."

"Um ..." I glance up after arranging small piles of napkins around the trays. "He ..." I can barely bring myself to say it. "Lapped up her blood."

"Kelsey picked out an explicit novel last year, and everyone loved it." Freya stands erect and parks her hands on her hips.

"It was a historical war romance, and the hero didn't go down on the heroine during her period."

"Drayken is a vampire, and it's appropriate for the genre."

I chuckle. "I'm not sure that's ever appropriate."

"Whatever. Hopefully, your pick will go over better than mine."

I feel confident my pick will rate higher than the vampire feasting on bloody—

Shaking my head, I wrinkle my nose. Nope. I can't even *think* about the words.

"Hello!" Brea and Piper arrive first, as usual. They're germophobic and want to fill their glasses and plates before everyone else contaminates the food.

Over the next few minutes, small clusters of mingling twenty-and-thirty-somethings snack and chat as everyone congregates on the rooftop. A line of sun umbrellas shields us from the fireball of death in the sky. It's still in the 90s, but hopefully, the temperature will dip another five degrees as we start our discussion.

"Okay. Let's take our seats and get started," I announce.

The small gathering, minus the new guy Eric, takes their places on the lined-up sofas separated by several long coffee tables filled with food and beverages and a few paperback copies of the book, some with sticky tabs marking spots in the first eight chapters.

"Let's start with our usual opening by going down the line and everyone giving their one-word first impression of the assigned chapters. I'll go first." I smile because this is, hands down, the best story I've read in a long time. "Gripping."

Everyone follows with a wide range of adjectives: intriguing, captivating, dynamic, sexy, emotional, intense, fascinating, engaging, and evocative.

They like it so far. Freya shoots me a smile and a nod. I'm off to a much better start than her cunnilingus vampire book. These are my neighbors, my friends, and my village. Of course, I want them to like my taste in books.

"Great. So I have three different topics to discuss tonight. Let's start with—"

The door to the right creaks open. Eric cringes. "Sorry I'm a few minutes late. I had to grab a quick shower." He sits across from me with his wet hair, prominent cheekbones, and perfect smile. I might have a tiny crush on Mr. Chivalrous. I inspect his ripped jeans, untied white sneakers, and tee that says "Fresh Out Of" with an image of two ducks at the end.

Yes. I definitely have a crush on him. If he were on one of my dating apps, I'd swipe right so fast my finger might break.

"We're just getting ready to discuss the prologue," I say.

"Wait! Eric must share his first impression of the book ... with one word." Freya smiles, passing two different bottles of wine in Eric's direction.

"Oh ..." He takes the red wine and fills a glass. "One word, huh?" His lips twist as he finds an empty spot to set the bottle on the table. "Redundant." He takes a sip of wine.

I narrow my eyes a fraction as a few other people chuckle. It's a joke. Right?

Eric shrugs. "Has that word already been used? Repetitive works too. I don't want to say predictable yet, but I'm a little suspicious that it's headed in that direction." When his gaze finds me, his smile doubles. "That's a magnificent dress, Anna. Red is your color." He winks.

Clearing my throat, I tighten my low ponytail, adjusting it slightly to keep my hair off my warm neck. Is he flirting with me after insulting my book choice? "Um ... what exactly did you find so repetitive about it?" I might be a little protective of my favorite author.

"The physical descriptions. The lead characters' hair and eye colors are mentioned seven times in eight chapters. Does the author think the readers aren't smart enough to retain those little details? If their physical descriptions were an integral part of the story—like a tattoo with a hidden meaning—then I can see why repeating that would serve a purpose."

"True." Brea nods. "Now that you mention it, it is a little overkill."

Clearing my throat again, I take a sip of wine and paste a smile onto my face. "I don't think it takes away from the story. If anything, it keeps the visuals fresh;

the characters stay vivid ... almost real in the reader's mind."

Eric shrugs. "It's just an opinion. No big deal."

Ignoring his brushoff, I continue, "Anyway ... the prologue. It appears Jasmine is being chased into the woods. Who do you think is chasing her?"

"Her cat. He's tired of eating off-brand food from a can."

Everyone laughs at Greg's comment, knowing he hasn't read a single word of the book. Mel, his girlfriend, drags him to the book club. Jasmine doesn't have a cat, and everyone else knows that.

"I think she's running from her boyfriend. In chapter three, she says he's been overprotective of her," Tricia offers the first logical explanation.

I've read the book, so hearing some of these early guesses is fun.

Spoiler alert—it's not the boyfriend.

Two other people agree it's the boyfriend. Several other people think it's the landlord who owns the farmhouse Jasmine's renting with her boyfriend.

"It's her mom."

The group laughs at Eric's response.

"The mom?" I chuckle.

"Sure." He shoves a chip into his mouth. "Just an early guess."

"Why do you think it's the mom?" Freya asks.

"I don't know. I read a lot of books, and it's hard to throw me off. This book feels ..." He shoves two more corn chips into his mouth while leaving me hanging with how the book feels to him.

"It feels what?" I tire of waiting.

"Sophomoric. If I'm wrong, if it's not the mom, *that* will surprise me."

"Drink up, everyone. There's plenty of wine." Freya passes more bottles of wine down the line.

"Moving on." I force myself to stop glaring at Mr. Shits All Over My Favorite Book. "Character development ..."

The good news? Everyone seems to like the characters—except Eric. He calls Jasmine weak and gullible, so I stop allowing him to share his opinions. By the end of the evening, I can't even look at him.

"Where do you want the empty wine bottles?" Eric asks as I toss dirty plates into a trash bag.

"Leave them. You don't need to help clean up." I avoid any chance of eye contact.

"I want to. So where do they go?"

Up your ass. All of them. You should shove them up your ass for being such a dick.

Chivalry, my ass.

"In that box by the door. I'll take them back to work to be recycled. Thank you, Eric. It's kind of you." Freya wraps her full lips around his ego and blows so hard I fear she'll pop him. "I'm going to grab some cleaner to wipe down the table, Anna."

"Okay," I mumble, brushing past Eric to set the trash by the door.

"Have I done something wrong?"

"Nope." I shuffle my flip-flop-clad feet over to the opposite end of the rooftop and start collapsing the sun umbrellas.

"Good. I was worried I somehow offended you; that would make me feel terrible." He starts at the opposite end, helping me collapse the umbrellas. "I'm getting my first shipment of tees in the morning. What time do you get coffee?"

"I don't go for coffee on Wednesdays."

"Noted, but tomorrow is Friday."

"I'm not drinking coffee at the moment. It's too hot."

"I bet they can make iced coffee."

We meet in the middle at the last two umbrellas, forcing me to acknowledge him with an actual glance. "A date? Are you asking me on a coffee date?"

"Definitely." White teeth peek out from his quirked lips while his eyes wander down my body.

"Are you checking me out?"

"Affirmative." He chuckles after ogling my legs beneath the red dress that supposedly is my color.

"I'm not interested."

His head cocks to the side. "In coffee or letting me check you out?"

"Listen, I'm not okay with how you tried to decimate our book club tonight. After just eight chapters, your negative and speculative views of the book were awkward and insulting."

He squints, parting his lips a fraction. "O—kay. I offended you?"

I shake my head, scrunching up my face. "No. Of course not. Other people are enjoying the story. So when you're *so* critical of the book, they feel judged."

"Judged how?" He slides his hands into his front pockets.

"Like you think they don't have good taste in books. When, after tonight, I think you're the one who doesn't know a good story when it's right in front of your face."

"Whoa ..." He steps backward as if I gave him an invisible shove. "It's just an opinion about a book. I'm not judging anyone. Diversity is beautiful. If everyone had the same taste, life would be boring."

"Well ..." I start my rebuttal, but how do I argue with "diversity is beautiful?" Instead, I frown. Really ... it's a pout.

"If you think my opinions are too disruptive, I won't return to the book club. My sincerest apologies. But I still want to have coffee with you."

He's so ... *Ugh!* I don't know. Why does he have to wear cute shirts and say profound things that make it hard to stay mad at him? He's supposed to be the last good guy. I think I *need* him to be that guy.

"Dating someone who lives in my building is a bad idea." It's not a lie, but it's also not my hard and fast rule.

Rubbing his kissable (yes, they're kissable) lips together, he nods slowly. "I see. So let's have coffee, and it won't be a date."

"I pay for my coffee, right?"

He smirks. "Anna, I'm going to make you pay for your coffee, even if we call it a date."

My jaw unhinges to say something. What? I'm not sure. Should I be offended? Should *he* be offended that I was presumptuous? "Now you're just being a dick."

His gaze drifts to my legs again for a few seconds. "Yeah, well ... I'm fresh out of ducks to give about you thinking I'm a dick. I'm not. You'll see." He winks before pivoting and sauntering to the stairs.

"Feel free to take that bag down to the dumpster," I say.

"Nah ... that might fall under the buying-you-a-coffee level of kindness. And I'm not going there."

"Asshole," I whisper with an unavoidable grin.

CHAPTER THREE

Eric didn't give me a specific time to meet him for coffee, so I'm choosing my usual time, not caring if we have coffee. Sort of not caring. He has an innocent arrogance. An oxymoron? Probably, but it's the best label.

"You're late." Eric smirks, his shaggy, damp hair partially sweeping across his forehead as he looks edible, propped up against the counter with his legs crossed and a paper cup in one hand.

"We didn't set a time. I can't be late."

Finn slides a to-go cup toward me as I swipe my debit card. He knows my usual drink and my usual time. I love Des Moines' East Village.

"You look pretty." Eric manages to type something into his phone with one hand before slipping it into his pocket and pinning me with those deviant eyes and an ornery smile.

"Pretty? Huh ... I don't think anyone has ever said

those three words to me. It's a little old-fashioned, don't you think?"

"Nah. *Pretty* is a timeless compliment. Cute as a bug's ear is a little dated. 'The brightness of her cheek would shame those stars ...' if you're into Shakespearean compliments. Or are you partial to the eighteenth century? 'Sweet lady, your virtues have so strangely taken up my thoughts, that therein they encrease and multiply in abundant felicity.'"

My thoughts trip over themselves. Eric's quoting Shakespeare and eighteenth-century pick-up lines?

Be still, my beating heart.

"I'm trying to be polite since you didn't think I was polite at book club," he says.

I slide my debit card into my phone holder before picking up my coffee cup. "Why sugarcoat it now?" It's too much effort to feign anger, so I set my toothy grin free. I have never met anyone quite like Eric Steinmann.

"Fine. You look fuckable."

I cough, thankfully, before taking a sip of coffee.

Finn sniggers behind me as I follow Eric.

"I'll take pretty," I mumble. "Where are you going?"

He pushes open the door and holds it for me. I'd expect nothing less.

"Your tardiness means we must drink our coffee at my store since my shipment will arrive soon."

"I have to be at work in an hour."

"Good thing my store is right here." He walks ten

steps to the right. "A two-minute walk from the boul-dering gym or a twenty-second bike ride. Correct?"

I chase his intoxicating spicy scent like a dog would chase bacon with legs into the retail space filled with cubed shelves and a few round racks. Eric hands me his cup, and I take it after a second of hesitation. He tips one of the box displays on its side and retrieves the coffee from me before sitting on the display and nodding for me to sit beside him. Then he stares out the window at the reserved parking space for the impending delivery.

"So ..." I take a seat. "Are you originally from Des Moines?"

"Kansas City." He sips his coffee.

"What brought you here? Surely people in Kansas City buy T-shirts."

"Followed a girl to law school at Drake."

"Oh ..."

"Don't worry. If this were a date, which it's not, I wouldn't be cheating on her. We broke up."

"Sorry. What happened? Did you trash her favorite book?"

His head swivels toward me. "Funny."

It's not, but I won't rehash that right now.

"No. We fought about other things, like her deci-sion to smoke because it soothes her nerves. My grandpa died from that shit. I couldn't figure out how someone in their twenties with a high IQ could start smoking. One night, she had too much to drink and tried seducing me after smoking half a pack of cigarettes. I pushed her away because nicotine doesn't get me hard. She screamed at me and told me to get the hell out. So I did."

I nod slowly. "Why didn't you go back to Kansas City?"

"Finn."

"Coffee shop Finn?"

He nods. "He's my cousin and told me about this open space."

"Have you always wanted to open a T-shirt shop?" I playfully lean into him and quickly right myself because he's a slippery guy. I can't fall for his charm when I know he has such poor taste in books.

Eric has a gleam in his eyes. "Yep," he whispers, leaning to the side to nudge me the way I nudged him, but he lingers like he wants me to know he didn't miss my inadvertent flirting. "Since I was a wee little thing, all I could think about was a store full of T-shirts."

Biting the inside of my cheek, I nod. It's ... an interesting dream.

He sits up straight and chuckles. "I'm just kidding."

I roll my eyes and smirk before sipping my coffee and returning my focus to the street.

"Thanks to successful parents," he runs his hand through his hair, "I've had the luxury of exploring my options in life without feeling a financial burden. They're waiting for me to sow my wild oats and return home to take over the family business. So this store adventure is nothing more than my love of T-shirts with crazy sayings. I have the rare and much-appreciated luxury of opening a business without worrying about its success."

"I see. You're just a spoiled rich kid."

"Guilty." He grins. "But the good kind. What about you? Are you a professional rock climber?"

"No. Not even close. I'm in charge of marketing. That's my degree. I like it here, and it's affordable city living. My parents live in West Des Moines, so I'm an Iowa girl."

"Who loves reading?"

"Yes. Books are life," I declare with a sharp nod.

"Books aren't life. People use them to escape life, learn things that will help them achieve success, or find new ways to cope with life. *Life* is what happens outside the bound story. Life isn't the letters on the page; it's what inspires those words."

Damn! A well-spoken, probably well-read man. I'm a little turned on. This crush I have on him is going to the next level. "See! If you could bring this level of insight to the book club, I wouldn't have had to kick you out." I laugh, giving his arm another playful nudge. Maybe I'm in heat. What else explains my need to rub up against him?

Eric angles his body toward mine. "I didn't realize someone had officially removed me from the club."

"Uh ... yeah. You're out." I hide my grin behind my coffee cup.

"For being honest? Is honesty *not* the best policy?"

Staring out the window to keep him from seeing

the pleasure I'm getting from our conversation—from *him*—I sigh. "Compassion should trump honesty when supposed honesty is an opinion and not a fact, like a doctor delivering a cancer diagnosis. They can infuse as much compassion as possible, but the truth will hurt, and it's also necessary. Book club should not feel like a cancer diagnosis."

"What happened to the art of debating a good book? Isn't that part of the *discussion?*"

"Fine." I set my cup aside and kick my leg over to straddle the display while I cross my arms. "Let's *discuss* the things you said. It's not repetitive and redundant. And it's definitely not sophomoric."

A growing smile takes over his face just before he throws his leg over the display to mirror me. "The dialogue is above average." He reaches for my shirt, and I stiffen while he pulls a hair from it. "But the narration is clumsy and disconnected," he says while releasing the hair to the floor.

"There's a ton of description."

He shakes his head. "Purple prose and too much showing instead of telling. The book could double in dialogue and cut out half of the filler shit, and it would be a better story."

"Seriously? What makes you such an expert?"

That stupid smirk. *Gah!* I hate it and love it in equal parts. I love a good debate about anything except my favorite book.

He shakes his head. "Nothing. I've just read many books."

I blow out another breath, sending my sun-bleached, partially grown-out bangs away from my face.

"You're cute when you're mad." He taps the toe of my sneaker with his before sipping his coffee.

I glare at him, unsure if I'm angry because he doesn't like my book or because I'm attracted to him despite his terrible taste in books. "I'm not cute when I'm mad."

"Fine. Let's go with fuckable again. You look fuckable when you're mad."

I will not smile. Nope. There's no way I'm taking the bait. He's insulted my favorite book. And books are my friends, so I must defend my friend. "You're crude and ... and ..." *Dammit! I've got nothing!* "A real *chivalrous* gentleman would have offered to pay for my coffee. And *stop* looking at me like that!" He's snake-charming my nipples. This shit needs to stop. I'm losing my mind.

"You're beautiful too."

I roll my eyes. "I have to get to work," I say, while grabbing my coffee and my last resolve before leaving.

❚❙═╱❙❙❙═╲❙❙❙

EVERYONE CRAWLS under my skin the rest of the day until I'm forced to apologize to my coworkers before leaving work. Freya greets me with a huge grin when I walk into our two-bedroom apartment, tossing my keys on the gray quartz island.

"Why the look?" I mumble.

She sets her phone on the sofa and sashays to the island's opposite end, eyeing me with a suspicious smirk the whole way. "Look what our new neighbor dropped off."

I glance at the card in her hand, taking a few steps closer before snatching it from her hold. It's a *five-hundred*-dollar gift card to Finn's café.

"He must have slid it under our door before I got home. Here's the note." She hands it to me.

Anna,

Thanks for hosting the book club. It was the most donnish experience I have enjoyed in a long time. Think of this as a hostess gift. Regards, Eric

"He's hot and generous." Freya fans herself.

"He's obnoxious."

And sweet.

And funny.

And sexy.

And a bunch of other annoying things.

"No. You don't get to be pouty because he was critical of your book pick. He's *one* person. Everyone hated my book pick, and you didn't see me unfriending anyone because of it. I think you're pissed because you're attracted to him. And now that he doesn't share your taste in books, you can't imagine riding his enormous cock. Your disappointment is understandable, but don't let it impede a good thing."

I laugh and shake my head while she animatedly makes her case by stroking her imaginary dick.

"You don't know that his cock is big. And my attraction to him doesn't matter because I'm not getting involved with someone who lives in my building. *And* ... I don't care that he has terrible taste in books. I don't. Really ... whatever. I'm over it."

"Good idea. Get over it and then get under him."

I scrunch my nose. "You get under him."

"I'm engaged."

I grab a bag of popcorn from the cabinet next to the fridge and toss it into the microwave. "You're engaged to a man you've never met. And he keeps making excuses for not moving here. Seriously ... will you have an online wedding and consummate your marriage with a string of dirty texts or via video chatting?"

"I'm so disappointed in you." She tips up her chin. "I thought you were more of a romantic than that. A cheerleader for the underdogs."

I hand her the gift card. "I'm your biggest cheerleader. When your Latino lover arrives ... coffee is on me."

She smirks, picking up the gift card and sliding it into her pocket. "I did provide the wine."

CHAPTER FOUR

I MAKE it a week without seeing my new neighbor. Granted ... I've had to find a new place to get coffee, and avoiding him near the bike racks has been total luck.

"Hot guy alert." Kenzie pops her head into the back office of the bouldering gym as I work on the employee newsletter.

I crane to see past her before jerking back into a hunched position. My luck just ran out. "He's my new neighbor, and don't tell him I'm here."

She laughs. "Too late. He already asked for you."

"I'm busy."

"He wants to hire you to spot him."

"What?" My nose wrinkles while I focus on the computer screen.

"You know ... make sure he doesn't get injured if he falls."

"I know what it means. We don't do that. You only spot when you're outdoor climbing."

"Fine. I'll tell him that you don't want to do it. Is that what you want me to tell the hot guy?"

"Um ... *yes*." I squint at her. What's her deal?

She grumbles and pivots. A few seconds later, she returns. "Dude! He's offered to pay a thousand dollars an hour for you to spot him."

"The answer is still no." I continue typing.

"If I tell Linda you said no to the gym making a thousand dollars an hour to spot him, she will fire you."

My gaze slides to the side, burning a massive hole into Kenzie's forehead. Linda would not fire me. She knows the safety concerns and his ridiculousness in asking for that service. He could crush me, and it's not like he's bouldering outside where he can miss the crash pad and crack open his head on a jagged piece of granite.

"You heard her say we fell short of our membership renewal goal last month."

The answer is still no, but Kenzie's having a brain fart and can't see she's being played.

"Spoiled..." I shut my computer "...little..." I shove the desk chair back "...rich kid." I stand, balling my hands.

Kenzie bites her lips together. "He seems nice. And hot. Did you not focus on his body or that smile? Or the hair?"

He hates my favorite book, and I bet he hates kittens and puppies, too—a total monster.

"Eric." I don't offer so much as a twitch of my lips that could be mistaken for a smile.

"Hey, neighbor." He glances up from the waiver form on the tablet before him.

"Hi, *neighbor*," I say through my teeth. "Spotters aren't used for indoor climbing. Your assumption that we would do that is *sophomoric* at best."

His finger continues to tap the tablet screen. "I have a thousand dollars ... maybe even two ... that says you're spotting me today."

Kenzie's gaze ping-pongs between us, and I give her a nod to do something else.

Resting my forearms on the counter, I narrow my eyes and lower my voice. "What's your angle?"

"My angle?" He presses *submit* on the waiver and tries to slice through my distrust with his signature perfect-teeth grin.

"What do you want from me? Even spoiled rich kids like you have *some* ulterior motive for paying for a nonexistent service beyond just the fact that you can."

"I love that you call me a kid." He rests his arms on the counter, mirroring me, forcing me to step back if I don't want him in my personal space. Which I don't.

Not in my personal space.

Not in my book club.

Not in my apartment building.

And not in my place of business.

"Is this..." his eyes narrow when he cocks his pretty little head to the side "...about the book?"

"Pfft ... don't be ridiculous. Your opinion means nothing to me."

"Great. Then let's do this. I expect less talking and more climbing for a thousand an hour."

I murder him twenty ways in my head. Pull out his Shawn Mendes hair. Kick in his sparkly teeth. Jab sharp objects into his wandering eyes. And slap the grin right off his face. "I'm going to stand at a safe distance with my hands in my pockets. If you fall, I'm not moving an inch. It's called watching ... not spotting."

He smirks. That's it—just that infuriating smile.

I follow him to the cubbies.

"How long have you climbed?" he asks while shoving his bare feet into his climbing shoes.

I return a blink. That's all he's getting from me—a slow, lifeless blink.

"I've climbed since I was fourteen," he says.

Here you go, buddy ... another no-shit-given blink.

"Thanks for asking." His kissable—

Gah! NOT kissable.

His dry, cracked, pus and blood-oozing lips curl into a psycho's smirk.

Much better, Anna. Stay focused.

"I didn't ask." I shrug.

"But you should have. It's the polite thing to do, and that's how conversations work." Eric stands a solid six inches taller than me.

His proximity forces me to smell him. I wish he smelled like an old gym bag, but he doesn't. My nose could easily bury itself in the crook of his neck and get high off his subtle spicy scent.

Instead of breathing through my nose, I part my lips and read the words on his T-shirt. *If you were a bouldering problem, I'd flash you.*

"I wore this shirt for you."

My eyes hurt from rolling them so much. "More climbing, less talking."

Over the next hour, Eric flashes every problem in the gym. We need to set more challenging routes.

"You're an ass," I murmur as he peels off his shoes.

"Why am I an ass? I didn't fall on you ... not once. And I didn't talk to you."

"You paid a thousand dollars to force me to watch you show off ... easily climb every single problem."

He closes his chalk bag. "It's my mating dance."

My jaw clenches. After a few seconds, my lips quiver as the life-or-death need to not laugh, not show my amusement, becomes unbearable. "I have to get back to work." I speed walk to the empty yoga room and hide around the corner, covering my mouth to hide my smile and stifling my laughter.

"So you *did* like my mating dance."

I jump, angling my body away from Eric's while keeping my hand over my face. My pulse doubles, and my heart beats so loudly I bet he can hear it march to the metronome of my attraction to him. "Go home. I'm not impressed by ... by anything about you."

"No? Then why are your cheeks so pink?"

"They're not." I press my palms to my damp face.

I glance up.

Shit.

Our gazes meet in the mirror.

My eyes constrict into tiny slits at his reflection, and he always wears an expression like he's ruminating about something I just said or did.

"Anna, they've been pink since I removed my shirt halfway through climbing all the routes." He shrugs. "Don't be embarrassed. If you took off your shirt, I'd overheat too."

"You are so arrogant."

"You liked my mating dance, didn't you?"

Why? Why must he say that? It's impossible to maintain a straight face when he says mating dance. "Please stop saying that." I bite my lips together.

He saunters toward me, backing me into the corner of the room. "Mating dance?" Mr. Arrogant cocks his head a fraction, lips turning to a wolfish grin.

"Stop." My whole face contorts to hide my amusement. My legs squeeze together to hide other reactions to him, his bare chest, low-hanging climbing pants, and

…

No!

"I've wanted to kiss you since the day we met."

"Shut up," I murmur just above a whisper, a little breathy as I dip my chin toward my chest.

"We were destined to reach this moment. The flirty glances, the sexual banter, the coffee date, you and your not-so-subtle nudging me, and my *mating dance.*"

Laughter spills from deep in my chest. I can no longer hold it together. "Go. Home! You're an idiot. The opposite of sexy is a man saying the words 'mating dance' unless he's narrating something for National Geographic." I cover my face and shake my head.

Eric lowers his voice. "The skittish female Homo sapiens' face flushes as she drops her chin to disguise her attraction to the rather well-endowed male as he makes his advance. She's stubborn but not immune to his mating dance. It's only a matter of time before he imparts his scent onto her, marking her for life."

I wipe the tears from my eyes. What is this? I don't understand what he's doing. It's ridiculous.

When I meet his gaze, he wets his lips. "Come to the forest with me to forage for food together."

"You're delusional."

"Then just pizza tonight. The place across the street from our building. Seven o'clock."

I know better. I really do. Yet, I find myself nodding. "No rubbing your scent on me."

He holds up his hands and takes a step backward. "I won't touch you, but it's not my fault if you're rolling all over me by the night's end. You've already shown your hand. You *like* when we're touching ... *rubbing* ... rolling is the next step."

"There's a zero percent chance of that."

"I guess we'll see." He winks before disappearing around the corner.

CHAPTER FIVE

"Finally! I knew you liked him." Freya shows way too much excitement over my dinner plans with Eric.

"I like him a little, but mostly he annoys me. I won't be gone long." I deposit my phone into my handbag.

"I won't wait up for you." Freya props her feet on the coffee table and turns on the TV.

"See you in about an hour." I slip on my yellow wedge sandals and look in the entry mirror at my fitted denim capris and plain white tee—an excellent choice for eating pizza with *red* sauce.

"Mmm-hmm ..."

I shake my head at Freya and open the door to our apartment. "Oh my god ..." I whisper.

"What?" Freya mumbles.

I gulp. "Uh ... nothing." I shut the door behind me, mouth agape at the trail of flower petals in a rainbow of colors, starting at my door and leading to the stairway.

A few areas are scattered; probably other residents have traipsed through the trail. I follow it to the stairs, lobby, out the door, and straight across the street to the pizza place.

Yes, they are in the street as well. I'm not sure how he managed it, but the trail of petals continues into the restaurant and to a table near the door—thankfully—where my arrogant, book-hating neighbor waits for me.

Looking ... well, never mind. I'm not going to obsess over how he looks.

Sex. He looks like sex—the ultimate scratch to every "itch" I've ever had.

I have self-control. This won't be an issue.

"Thanks for following the dress code." He grins.

What to address first ... His plain white tee? His denim jeans that are the same shade as mine? Or his silly yellow canvas shoes? What were the chances?

For one second, can we discuss the bouquet of stems on the table? Petal-less flowers.

If he's going for original, he's beaten every other guy in the field.

"You have a mess to clean up," I say while keeping a straight face even though it's hard to do around Eric.

"Don't ever surrender." He hands me a menu. "Promise me you'll always make me work for it."

It's hard not to surrender to that smile.

"Work for what?" I hide behind the menu before he melts me into a puddle of mush with one look.

Fucking mating dance ...

"You."

Make him work for me? *Jesus* ...

"What kind of pizza do you like?" I've suddenly spiked a fever, so I use my menu to fan myself.

"I'll eat absolutely anything." If he could say that casually while studying his menu instead of running his gaze along my face to my chest, I might be able to concentrate on things like mushrooms, pepperoni, and Roma tomatoes.

Instead, my mind goes south where I cross my legs and do *not* think of things he could eat that aren't on the menu. I'm in trouble, and I hate being in trouble. I believe physical attraction is a human flaw. Our species is too intellectual to be swayed by a nice body and a killer smile. And hormones ... they're poison.

"Not me. There's a short list of things I'll put in my mouth."

He chuckles at my attempt to blend in with my menu again. "I don't doubt that."

"What if we just do cheese?" I slap my menu shut. "Plain cheese. Nothing crazy. Quick. Easy."

Eric sets his menu beside the naked bouquet and drums his fingers on the table. "Quick and easy, huh?"

"Stop." I shake my head. "Stop making everything so sexual."

He presses a hand to his chest as if I'm the offensive one. "I think the first person to use the word 'sex' is the one being sexual."

I blink at his straight face for several seconds. "I apologize. That was presumptuous of me." I lift the menu to cover my face again, and he does the same. We're playing a weird game of peek-a-boo.

"I mean ... I'll just throw this out there and let you mull it over," he says.

I lower my menu an inch.

"If you're easy, I can probably be quick."

Biting my lips together, I snort and retreat to the safe space behind my menu.

The waitress arrives at our table. I hand her our menus before she can ask if we're ready to order. "Medium supreme, a pitcher of whatever your best beer on tap is, and an order of hot wings ... the spicier, the better."

She smiles. "You got it."

Eric clucks his tongue several times. "Anna Banana ... aren't you full of surprises."

I lean back in my chair and give him my best flirty expression that involves lip biting and my gaze lingering on his kissable ... yup, I'm thinking it ... *kiss-able* lips. If I can keep my mind off his regrettable taste in books, I can focus on things we can do to scratch itches and not ruin our neighborly relationship.

"My sister would love your grand gesture." I nod to the flower stems.

"Oh?" Eric tilts his head. "Is that your way of saying I should be dating your sister?"

"Not even close. She's married with two kids. But her husband buys her flowers all the time."

"She loves flowers. I see." He eyes the couple leaving the restaurant.

I laugh. "She hates flowers *because* he gives them to her all the time. Red roses, to be specific."

"Poor guy. I bet he gives them to her, thinking that one day if he dies first, she will tell their grandkids how Grandpa gave her red roses, and every time he did, she fell in love with him all over again."

"I love that you're defending him."

"I love that you're having dinner with me tonight." Eric Steinmann uses one of those industrial-sized push brooms to sweep me off my feet. "Do you have any other siblings that would love my grand gesture?"

"Nope. Just one sister." I fiddle with the paper wrap holding my napkin and silverware.

"I'm envious. I'm an only child."

"Because you were too perfect or a total terror?"

"You know the answer to that." His eyes narrow.

"I don't. Enlighten me."

"Slept through the night from the day I was born. Potty trained myself a week later. First job by the time I was two ..."

"Stop." I giggle.

His contagious grin doubles like his far-fetched story of Super Baby. "Actually, I was eight weeks premature. My mom suffered severe postpartum depression. I did everything late in life ... walk, talk, potty train, read, and make friends. Go figure. The couple, who never wanted kids, had an unplanned pregnancy and a difficult child."

"Do you want kids?"

"Of course. How many should we have?"

Heat fills my cheeks. "No hand-holding. No first kiss. We're just going to plan a family?"

"You're a traditionalist?" His teeth drag along his lower lip while his chin dips into an easy nod. "That's cool." The legs of his chair screech along the floor as he stands.

My eyes widen while he leans over the small table, reaches for my hand, and gently takes it while he presses his lips to mine.

I freeze—all thoughts obliterated, next breath stolen, heart stilled.

He reverses just as quickly, taking a seat and scooting his chair toward the table. "I'd like at least two ... and maybe a third one that's unplanned—conceived in a moment of untethered passion."

I slowly rub my lips together, feeling his kiss that reached far beyond my mouth.

"Have uh..." I'm breathless and incurably flustered "...you opened your shop?"

"You'd know the answer if you weren't avoiding my cousin's cafe—if you wouldn't have given Freya the gift card."

"Her fiancé lives in another country, and she's not had sex in two years." I forge ahead with this new subject because I have not and will not be formulating coherent thoughts about that kiss and *our kids* anytime soon. Or ever.

He coughs. "She might need more than a gift card for coffee."

"For sure." I laugh, tucking my hair behind my ear.

The waitress drops off our beer, and I watch her return to the counter to grab our plates and basket of wings. After she leaves again, I pour beer for both of us. "Do you have your apartment decorated?"

"Absolutely." He brings his beer to his lips and smirks. "My mom sent a snake plant. I have a sofa and a coffee table."

"You're a minimalist. Nice."

His laughter wraps around my chest, warm and comforting. "Bare minimum."

"There's a new antique store off Walnut Street. Want to check it out with me this weekend?"

"A second date?" His eyebrows lift.

I shrug, giving him my best coy expression.

"You probably should make a good inspection of my apartment before we go shopping for furnishings. Maybe after dinner, you could take a look around." He cups his beer and drums his fingers on the table with his other hand.

And that look on his face? It says I'm in trouble. Eric Steinmann isn't anything I'll be able to quit without therapy.

After dinner, we exit the restaurant hand in hand, and he guides me down the sidewalk. I don't know where we're going, and I don't care. I point to all the shops he should check out when they're open. He presses the buttons for the crosswalks, worming our way to the other side of East Village, where there's a skating park filled with skaters, kids at the adjacent park, and a crowd of people milling around by the bridge and walking dogs under the bright lights.

Eric stops to push a child on the swing as their mom struggles to soothe her other child in a carrier. She thanks him with exhaustion on her face.

His hand returns to mine, and we mosey along the trail. "I never imagined liking Des Moines as well as Kansas City."

"But?" I gaze up at him.

He gives me a quick sidelong glance before returning his attention to the skaters. The hint of a grin bends his lips. "But it's growing on me. Tonight, I'd say it's growing on me *a lot*." He squeezes my hand.

We stop near a crowd of people watching two guys on skateboards tearing it up. They're wicked good. I tense up every time they leave the ground and relax again when they land in one piece. Eric chuckles at my cringes. When our gazes meet, smiles mirrored, he wets his lips and walks me back a few feet, so we're away from the crowd.

My skin tingles and my heart knocks around in my chest when he slides his hand along my neck and kisses me. The kiss ends too soon, but he keeps his head ducked while sweeping his gaze over my face and kissing me again. This time, his tongue flicks my lip, and I relax, opening for him. His other hand cups my cheek, and we moan simultaneously, making me grin and break the kiss.

Dropping my chin, I press my fingertips to my lips. Are people staring at us making out?

"I think it's time for you to inspect my apartment ... you know, to give me decorating tips."

I force myself to look at him even though I know my face is flushed along with the rest of my skin. Offering him nothing more than a quick nod, he wraps an arm around my waist, sliding his fingers into my back pocket while we make our way to his apartment.

When we have to wait for the lights to change at crosswalks, Eric turns and kisses me. Each kiss escalates. We are a tangled mess of greedy lips and wandering hands when we reach our floor.

A long walk has never been foreplay for me until tonight.

Sex on a first date has never been my style until tonight.

Public indecency has been a hard limit for me ... until tonight.

At every intersection where we had to wait for the light, I wanted Eric to go further.

Sex against the light pole? Honestly, I might have let him.

He stabs his key at the lock with our mouths remaining fused. It takes several attempts—probably because I have the button to his jeans flicked open, and my fingers are teasing his abs just above his briefs. We stumble into his dark apartment.

"The book club book ..." My words come out breathy. "Did you finish it?"

Where did that come from?

I internally scold myself. How does my brain go

there when every other body part is laser-focused on getting out of these clothes?

I feel his lips along my neck curl into a smile. "No."

"If you finished ... you could like it, right? There's a chance you could change your mind. Right?"

Why? Just *why* am I still talking?

Eric has my body pressed to the wall, legs around his waist.

My hands are in his hair.

His fingers grip my butt to move me against him.

And I'm ... asking about a book.

"Um ..." He chuckles before opening his mouth, hot tongue flicking the skin along my neck.

"Just ..." I tip my head to give him better access. I curse the clothes between us. I've never wanted a guy inside of me so badly. Yet ... I'm still talking about that fucking book. "Just tell me it's not entirely impossible."

He carries me to the bedroom. His fingers flick the button to my capris when my feet reach the floor, making breathing difficult.

"Eric ..." I need his answer, maybe not as much as other things ... but I still need it, nonetheless.

His hand slides into my panties, and he moans. Yep ... I can be this wet between my legs *and* think about a book.

"I'd say ..." The pad of his middle finger stops just shy of my clit. "Anything feels possible at this point." He ducks his head to kiss me, but I turn my head. He smirks. Taking advantage of his proximity, I run my fingers through his hair and kiss his cheek and stubbly jawline, dragging my lips to his earlobe, eliciting a soft moan.

I peel off his shirt and take a moment to admire him—his mussed hair, taut abs, and open fly.

"Anna, you're going to give me that mouth."

With a sly grin, I gaze at him while discarding my shirt ... and bra.

His hands curl into tight fists at his side when I step toward him, pressing my lips to his sternum. "I'll give you nothing until I'm ready," I say, gazing up at him.

He grips my jaw with one hand, his face soft and relaxed while his thumb slides along my lips. "That's my line, Anna." That playful sparkle in his eyes transforms into something wicked, sending a chill along my skin, two seconds before he shoves me onto the bed. I laugh, but it evaporates when he slides off his jeans and briefs in one smooth motion. I don't even pretend not to stare at his erection bobbing like a heavy spring while he retrieves a condom from his nightstand and rolls it on.

Eric displays too much patience ridding me of the rest of my clothes. He kisses my ankle, leg, knee, and inner thigh. I spread my legs an inch or two. Each breath that passes my lips sounds a little more ragged.

Kiss me there. Kiss me there. KISS ME THERE!

I grab his hair. He chuckles, biting the skin along my hip, entirely skipping a particular area.

"Eric ..." I try to force him to go in reverse.

"I'll give you nothing ... until I'm ready."

"Bastard," I whisper. "Ouch!"

He bites my nipple. "Try again." His tongue laps over it once before his lips creep up my neck.

"You're evil." I narrow my eyes and then jerk my head when he goes for my lips again.

His hand slides between my legs, burying two fingers inside me, sending my back arching off the bed as I gasp. He withdraws his fingers and pushes his erection between my legs, filling me in one hard thrust.

It's nice. *Really* nice. I-can't-breathe nice.

I lift to meet him, but he angles just enough to keep me from feeling one ounce of friction while he sets a steady pace.

While he sucks my nipples and teases them with his teeth.

While he gives up on trying to kiss me.

While his hand hooks my leg and lifts it toward my chest, sending him deeper.

Touch me. Touch me lower. Kiss me. Kiss me lower.

I have a clit. How can he ignore it? My clit will *not* be ignored!

My lips need his. My tongue keeps wetting them, readying them.

"Kiss me ..."

"I'm good." His face tenses as he speeds up his pace.

I attempt to wriggle beneath him, to find friction. He's the worst.

The. Worst.

I'm not suggesting every man I've had sex with has

been an expert with the female anatomy, but they've attempted (even if it was inaccurate and clumsy) to find that magical little nub.

How can one guy have so much physical appeal and potential and waste it by being bad at sex? *This* is why I don't screw men who live in my building. From now until the time that one of us moves out, it will be awkward. He will see me and smile like he's all that, but I'll know the truth. And the most I will be able to offer him is a cringe before averting my gaze and running in the opposite direction.

"Fuck!" I wince. "Stop biting my nip—"

Oh. Sweet. Baby. Zebras ...

Eric kisses me like God stopped by and gave him a tutorial on kissing a woman. At least, I assume God would be good at kissing. Things to think about later ...

My fingers claim his hair because I will physically harm him if he stops kissing me. Eric engulfs every inch of me with his body, bringing all of my senses to life as his hips prove they know about the special little clit. He hits it just right every time.

"Eric ... Fucking ... Steinmann!" My mouth rips from his, my head lulling to the side while I claw the mattress with one hand and his hair with my other hand.

"You're welcome," he chuckles, head buried in my neck, his rigid body incrementally relaxing on top of mine.

I can't argue. Nope. Not at all. He earned it. Man ... did he ever earn it.

After a few moments, he rolls us to our sides and grins while his gaze skates along my face, and he tucks a few strands of hair behind my ear. I barely catch my breath, and he kisses me. It's lazy yet deliberate. I fucking *love* kissing this man. Nothing makes me feel more desired than a slow kiss. I've never made out with a guy like this *after* sex. His hand presses to my cheek, tongue sliding against mine. Then that hand glides down my neck to my chest, where the pad of his thumb circles my nipple. And we do this for a while. Unrushed. Legs intertwined. Breaths mingling.

Eric's head inches away from mine, and he smiles. "When you're not angry, you're ineffably beautiful."

"Is that so?" Why does he have to be this irresistible? "When you're not insulting my favorite book, you're rather charming and sexy."

"Your favorite book?" He chuckles while his fingers tease my thigh. "If I say nice things about your favorite book, will it elevate me to a level beyond *charming and sexy*? I can't imagine it gets better than that."

I feather my hand along his chest to his back because I like touching him the way I think he likes touching me. "Perfect." I bite my lower lip and grin. "*Perfect* beats charming and sexy. You might be perfect if you like my favorite book. You have everything else. A contagious smile." My lips brush his. "Your irresistible eyes." I lift my gaze to said eyes. "Even your mating dance."

Eric's grin grows from something sexy and subtle to something so victorious that I feel it deep in my chest.

This—whatever *this* is—is different. He's different in the best possible way. I think I could like him more than I've liked any guy in a long time. Maybe ever.

Kissing my forehead, he murmurs, "For now, I'll settle for being sexy and charming." In the next breath, he saunters his naked ass to the bathroom.

What's that supposed to mean? He doesn't want to be perfect? He doesn't plan on liking my favorite book? An imposter's voice in my head whispers, "It's okay."

And it should be okay. It's. A. Book—fiction at that.

But ... it's not okay.

I slide into my capris, tug on my shirt, and gather my undergarments and shoes before tiptoeing to his front door. I hear the toilet flush as I ease it open and, just as quietly, shut it behind me before scurrying to my apartment. When I turn the corner into my bedroom, the hall light illuminates.

"What do we have here?"

I cringe at Freya with her messy red hair, boy shorts, black tank top, and *gotcha* expression. "Hey."

Her gaze locks on my arms cradling yellow sandals, a bra, and panties. "Looks like you bolted. Why did you bolt? Poor guy's going to feel rejected. Seriously ... I've never seen you home on the same night. Did he kick you out? Is he a weird sleeper? OCD? Bed hog? Did you start snoring?"

I roll my eyes. "No to all of the above."

"The sex was that bad?"

"No. Just..." I shrug "...the opposite."

Her eyes widen. "Oh ... my ... god. You like him.

Like ... *really* like him. He crawled under your skin, into your panties, and you didn't know what to do, so you left."

Shaking my head, I turn on my bedroom light and dump my stuff on the floor. "We live in the same building, and it just didn't make sense to stay all night." After plucking a nightshirt from my dresser, I change tops and shimmy out of my capris.

"So you said goodbye, and you didn't sneak out. Is that what you're saying?"

"It's late." I squeeze past her to the bathroom. "We had sex. It was good. I have to work tomorrow. End of story." I close the door.

"Are you going to have sex with him again?"

I plop onto the toilet and close my eyes. *God, I hope so.*

CHAPTER SIX

THE FOLLOWING DAY, I sneak out while Freya's in the shower. Checking the hallway through my door's peephole first, I dash to the stairs when I see the coast is clear.

"Morning, Anna." My neighbor, Peter, smiles as I unlock my bike from the rack.

"Good morning."

After securing my bag's crossbody strap over my torso, I walk toward the exit.

"Eric ... Fucking ... Steinmann!" Peter yells.

I freeze. I stop breathing. I'm not sure my heart is beating.

"Dude ... someone had a good night. Either the walls are much thinner than I realized, or you are some sort of god," Peter harasses Eric.

Praying for invisibility, I inch my bike toward the door without a glance backward.

"Anna Banana ... our neighbor heard you last night," Eric says.

No. He. Didn't.

He did not just call me out in front of Peter. That is the opposite of chivalrous. It's ... demonic.

I swallow my embarrassment and will away the flushing of my face as I glance over my shoulder just before reaching the door. "In your dreams, Steinmann."

Peter laughs, giving me an impish grin like he knows Eric is making shit up about me. I smile to confirm the ridiculousness of it before blowing a mock kiss to Eric Fucking Steinmann.

Dying—seriously *dying*—inside, I hop on my bike and bolt toward the cafe. I fully anticipate company, and within minutes, I'm greeted with a familiar spicy scent and soft lips at my ear as Eric steps in line behind me.

"Coffee, black. Meet me next door," he whispers, slipping something into my pocket and disappearing.

It takes me a few seconds to move. He's good at breathing down my neck, dissolving my panties, and turning my resolve into mush. Retrieving the twenty he slipped into my back pocket, I risk a glance back, but he's gone. Men like Eric should come with a warning because he's relentlessly ... everything.

Relentlessly sexy.

Relentlessly intriguing.

Relentlessly opinionated.

"Welcome. Let me know if I can help you with

anything." A young blonde with hair a little darker than mine smiles as I slip into Eric's T-shirt shop with our coffees.

"I'm here to see Eric."

"Oh! You must be Anna. He's in his office, and it's right back there beyond the restroom."

He told his employee about me. I wonder what he said.

"Thanks." I smile hesitantly before toting the two cups of coffee toward his office.

"Good morning. Shut the door." Eric leans back in his chair and props his feet up on the desk—red tennis shoes with white laces. From their pristine appearance, I'd say today is the first day he's worn them. They go well with his white shirt with red lettering: *I don't bite ... usually.*

"Black coffee." I shut the door, hand him his coffee, and dig out his change from the pocket of my gray skort.

"You can keep the change." He smirks right before taking a sip of his coffee.

"I'm good." I lay it on the desk and step back, but he snakes his hand around my bare leg, halting my retreat. "You're an awful man. The worst. I can't believe you called me out in front of Peter."

"Did you sleep well?" One hand inches up my leg while he casually sips coffee with his other.

I swallow hard when his fingers graze the bottom of my ass, and his thumb stops at the apex of my legs.

"Don't ignore me," I squeak, sounding more turned on than mad. But I'm not.

Okay, I am.

But fuck it. I'm mad too!

He shrugs. "I got more sleep than I planned on getting." Again, he sips his coffee like his other hand isn't planted in my personal space, like I'm not pissed off about the Peter incident.

I give up. "Oh yeah?" I attempt to mirror his casualness, but I'm standing next to him, not reclined in a chair, so it's a little trickier for me to come across as relaxed. "Well, things don't always go as planned."

"Mmm ... yeah. Well, I had plans to do things to a certain someone." His tongue slides along his bottom lip while his thumb teases the crotch of my skort.

"I have work." I take a cautious sip of my coffee, attempting to mask the slight strain in my voice.

Step back!

"I think this is a bad idea," I say.

Step back!

I have no willpower. What is wrong with me?

"Coffee is never a bad idea." His thumb moves to the same part of my body I felt sure he couldn't find last night—until he did find it, manipulated it, and destroyed me in the process.

Here I am ... refusing to step away because I welcome his destruction.

"We live in the same building. As a rule, I try to avoid setting up awkward situations with people I see on the regular. Like co-workers and neighbors."

"Awkward situations?"

I sip my coffee, nod as he sits up (hand still on my leg like it's stuck), and sets his cup on the desk. Then he places my coffee next to his before his other hand claims a matching position on my other thigh, pulling me between his spread legs.

"It's uh..." my fingers do their own thing, deeming it necessary to mess with his slightly damp hair "...bad news when things end, and we have to pretend they never happened, which is impossible to do. I have to watch you parade women in and out of your apartment, and you have to witness me coming home early in the morning, which means you'll know I spent the night at someone's place."

Pressing his lips together, gaze locked to mine, he nods slowly. "So you *do* stay the night ... just not at my place."

I roll my eyes. "I live in the building."

"Sorry ... did I not hear you say goodbye? Did I miss the note you left on the nightstand? We haven't shared phone numbers, so you didn't text me. You skittered out of my place in record time. Were you even fully dressed when you left?"

"Pfft ... of course I was dressed."

His gaze washes over my face, pausing on my cheeks. "Liar. You blush when you're turned on, and you blush when you lie. So either you're turned on or lying?"

Both.

I don't want to admit to either one.

"I didn't want to deal with what came next."

"*Next,* I planned on letting you read to me while my tongue explored ..."

I jump when his thumb shows me where he planned to let his tongue explore. A nervous laugh vibrates my chest. His hands slide down a few inches, and he lifts one leg, then the other, to straddle his lap.

"Good morning, Anna Black." He grins a second before kissing me. His confidence is its own entity.

The guy who kisses like the sun sliding up the east horizon, taking my breath away, is worthy of such confidence. I mean ... the sun owns the sky, deciding when to hide behind a thin layer of clouds and when to scorch the Earth.

"Jesus ..." I pull back, breathless, with my forehead propped against his and my fists clenching his shirt. "You can kiss."

"Yes. I can, but now I have work to do." He lifts me off his lap and smacks my ass. "Thanks for the coffee." He cups it with one hand like making a toast before taking a swig and opening his laptop.

I retreat a step, more like stumble, because that kiss has left me dizzy. "You're arrogant." I snatch my coffee.

Eric taps a few keys, keeping his gaze on the computer screen despite his lips curling a fraction. "Confident."

"Dismissive." I frown.

"Busy."

Tap. Tap. Tap.

He types away.

"A tease." I lift my bag onto my shoulder.

"Seductive. Go to work. Enjoy your freedom. When you're restrained to my bed tomorrow morning, you'll wish you made better use of your time today."

I infuse a pseudo-confidence into my laugh, posture, and wavering smile. "I might be restrained to a bed tomorrow morning, but it won't be yours." Forcing a tight smile, I exit with my chin up and extra sway to my hips as I leave his office.

I hear his faint chuckle followed by, "Oh, Anna ... Anna ... Anna ..."

CHAPTER SEVEN

Operation Avoid Eric Fucking Steinmann goes well for three full days after coffee and the most incredible kiss in his office. Why am I avoiding him?

Good question.

Things we can't resist are usually not good for us. Who lacks the willpower to avoid rainbow chard, five-mile jogs, and pap smears?

Eric is an ice cream sundae with extra chocolate and a jar of maraschino cherries on the first day of my period and the day I need to fit into a tight bridesmaid's dress.

I notice his bike in the rack when I get home late from work, so I keep a watchful eye, peeking around the corner to the stairs, tiptoeing up them, peering through the glass part of the door before easing it open, and using stealth mode to move past his door toward my apartment.

"Anna Black."

Dammit!

His door makes no noise, not the turn of the handle or a single creak of the hinges.

After a hearty gulp, I turn ninety degrees to see him, but not the full one-eighty like I intend not to continue to my door. "Hey. What's up?"

He scratches his scruffy jaw, and it's thicker scruff than the last time I saw him—three days with his over-abundance of testosterone equal bad news for my dry panties.

Eric rests his shoulder against the doorframe, propping the door open with his other shoulder. I instruct my eyes to stay above his nose, but they have issues with simple directions.

"Can you step inside here for a second?"

I shake my head.

"No?" He chuckles. "Why not?"

"I don't trust you."

"Me?" He jabs a finger into his chest. "What have I done to lose your trust? Or get the three-day ghosting, for that matter?"

"Nothing. I mean ... I've been busy. Working long hours."

"Not having coffee?"

"We have a Keurig. Just ... saving time and money." I shrug.

"Did Freya tell you I've knocked on your door numerous times? You're never home ... even when I know your bike is in the rack downstairs."

"Sometimes I walk. Sometimes I take an Uber to visit my parents."

"Sometimes you're hiding in your bedroom when I knock on your door."

Blinking several times, I formulate my next lie, but I'm too exhausted to think of a new one. "I don't know what you want," I whisper.

"What do you mean?"

"I mean, I don't know what this is. And I don't like that you live three doors down from me, and I have to dodge you like this."

He laughs, shaking his head. "Why are you dodging me?"

"Ugh!" I run my fingers through my hair. "Because I don't like the loss of control, and I don't like the polarity of emotions. One minute I like you; the next, I hate you. Then I'm back to liking you. Then you say something that rubs me wrong, and I'm back hating you. Then you open your door looking like..." I nod to his general sexiness "...*this*. And what am I supposed to do?"

He lifts an eyebrow.

I know I sound completely insane.

"Step inside for a minute."

"No way."

Eric smirks. "Why not? Are we still visiting that antique store tomorrow? Shouldn't you get a good look at my empty walls first?"

"Did you finish that book?"

Creases form along his forehead. "Books? We're talking about books again?"

I lift my chin and blink slowly. I know it shouldn't be a dealbreaker, but it is, and it's a character trait I can't overlook.

"No. You kicked me out of the book club, and I have no incentive to read it."

"I like the book. You seem to like me and don't want me ghosting you. There's your incentive to read it. And I'm busy. I can't go shopping with you tomorrow." I reverse my ninety-degree turn and take quick strides to my apartment door.

"Do I *have* to like the book? I said I was good with sexy and charming. Remember? Perfection is overrated."

Inserting the key, I close my eyes and clench my teeth but don't respond.

OVER THE NEXT WEEK, I don't go to great lengths to avoid Eric, nor do I intentionally put myself in his path. We pass occasionally, and he's always toting a copy of *The Last Person* and sporting a ridiculous smile.

"I've read the required chapters," he breaks our silence, following me up the stairs after we arrive home at the same time Friday afternoon. "Does that earn me entrance to the next book club?"

"Can you behave?" I open the door and continue as he picks up his pace behind me.

"At book club?" Eric snags my hand just before his door.

I try to pull away, but he tightens his hold, traps the book under his arm, and unlocks the door to his apartment.

"Of course, at book club. What else would I be talking about? Let go of me."

He drags me into his apartment, shuts the door, and tosses the book on the floor.

The audacity!

"What are you—"

He frames my face and kisses me, pressing my back to the door. "You look pretty today. Has anyone told you that?" he whispers.

Why can this man kiss so well? It's unfair, and it's dangerous. And I know this because I don't want to be caught in his web. And no. No one has told me I look pretty today.

"I got to the sex scene," he mumbles, sucking and biting along my ear and neck. "Now I know why you like that book so much."

Eric shoves his hand up my shirt, yanking my bra out of his way, just like Andrew does with Jasmine in the book. When our lips connect again, he carries me to the living room and sits on the sofa with me on his lap. It's Jasmine and Andrew.

He removes my shirt and his shirt. We kiss some more. Then I take the lead, shoving him back before crawling off his lap. I bite my lip while sliding out of my shorts and panties. He reclines more on the sofa, so most of his body engulfs it—just like Andrew.

I straddle his waist and lean forward, kissing my way up his chest to his neck ... and mouth.

"Higher," he whispers.

He did. He read it, and he liked it. I have never felt more turned on in my life. I grip the arm of the sofa with both hands while crawling up his body and rubbing myself against his torso.

Eric grips my hips. "Higher, baby," Andrew says those exact words to Jasmine as he guides her to straddle his face the way Eric guides me to straddle his face.

I moan, and my head tips back in ecstasy, just like Jasmine's does, when Eric's tongue makes its first swipe. It's teasing, seductive, and empowering to be above him like this, yet I surrender to his hold on me.

I officially love everything about Eric Steinmann. He's flirty and sexy. Smart and passionate. *Chivalrous.* And he says sweet things like, "You look pretty today," just seconds before nuzzling his face between my legs.

After I orgasm with his name on my lips and my fingers clenched in his hair, I waste no time repositioning myself between his legs.

"Baby, you don't have to ..." Eric gives me a weak protest with a drunken gaze, just like Andrew gave Jasmine.

"I know." I smirk while unzipping his jeans.

His first word is a sharp "fuck" as he tugs a fistful of

my hair. Minutes later, he repeats that word, but it's drawn out while his face contorts into something so beautiful, and it's precisely how I pictured Andrew.

Life isn't fiction; I get it, even if sometimes I don't like it. So I don't expect this to play all the way out. But … it does.

⁙⁙⁙

Early the following morning, I retrieve my scattered clothes and kiss his cheek while he sleeps. "I have to go," I whisper.

As I start to pull away, Eric cups the back of my head, our faces a breath apart. He grins. "I like you. I'm pretty sure I'm starting to like you a lot."

My heart soars.

"I like you *a lot* too."

He brushes his lips across mine. "Despite my obvious mating dance and charm that you've mentioned, I'm not a player."

"No?" I bite my lower lip.

"No." He pinches my nipple.

"Stop!" I giggle, trying to pull away.

"I don't want you dating anyone else."

"Eric, are you asking me to go steady? I think my parents did that in college."

He sits up, forcing me to stand straight. "I'm asking your vagina to go steady with my dick."

I snort while he stands, giving me a serious look and a single lifted eyebrow.

"You want me to be your girlfriend?"

"That's what I just said." He saunters to the bathroom.

"I gotta go. I'll consider your offer," I call when he's behind the bathroom door and I'm halfway to the front door.

After I've showered and made coffee and a huge breakfast, Freya shuffles her bare feet to the kitchen.

"Good morning." I smile, glancing up from my book. I've reread the chapters for the next book club discussion.

"Oh lord," she rolls her eyes and pours coffee. "I know that look. You had sex. Good sex. Afterglow sex."

I giggle. "May—be. Or maybe I'm just excited about the next book club."

Freya sets her coffee on the island and twists her wild hair into a bun while pinning me with an untrusting scowl. "I don't believe you. I know you love books, but they don't leave you looking like you rode the world's biggest dick for eight seconds."

My face cracks under my out-of-control grin. "Can you keep a secret? And I mean, legit keep a secret, not like your usual promise to keep a secret that ends in you blabbing it to everyone after two glasses of wine. I'm talking about the locked vault. Can you do that?"

"You're pregnant? Who's the baby daddy? I bet it's Carson. I can see him wanting to add a baby to the YouTube mix. The only thing that might get more views than Gilbert, the three-legged hero dog, is Gilbert, the three-legged hero dog with a baby. People love dogs and babies. I need a fucking dog and baby, so I can afford to bring my fiancé to me."

"It's not Carson's baby." I cover my mouth and shake my head. "No! I mean ... dammit! You have me so messed up with your crazy dog and baby scenario. I'm not pregnant. No baby. No baby daddy. I had sex again with Eric, but not just any sex. We had book sex. Jasmine and Andrew's sex. He read more of the book. And he liked it. *And* he wants us to be exclusive." I fold my hands at my chest to keep my limbs from flailing excitedly.

"What does that mean?" She wrinkles her nose.

"Exclusive?"

"No. Book sex?"

"He pulled me into his apartment last night, and he did to me what Andrew did to Jasmine. It was so *hot*."

"Oh ... that's ... weird."

I roll my eyes. "Not weird. Mind-blowing. The best sex I've ever had—times a million. It's not just the sex; it's the book!"

She sips her coffee, resting one hand on the island. "You can have mind-blowing sex with a guy and not be book soulmates. Please tell me you get that."

"Of course, I know that."

But I don't like to think about it.

"He's coming to the next book club. I won't be able to keep from blushing the whole time." My cheeks flush just from saying the words and thinking about the group discussing the erotic scene while Eric stares at me, knowing what we did last night.

Knowing that he thinks I'm pretty.

Knowing that he wants to be exclusive.

Knowing that he likes my favorite book.

Freya pops her lips several times, eyes wide. "Okay. Well, it should be interesting."

CHAPTER EIGHT

Eric: Wanna go on a date tonight?

I GRIN at his text while finishing the signup for the upcoming comp.

Anna: I do

Eric: Six?

Anna: Perfect

His invitation derails me for the rest of the day. I think I check off everything on my to-do list, but I'm not sure, and I don't care. At five, I clock out and fly down the street on my bike, desperate to get showered and look *pretty* for our date.

"Let me," Eric says behind me as I walk my bike toward the racks. He grins while lifting it into place for me.

"Such a gentleman."

His lips twist, head bobbing in a non-committal way. "Sometimes."

I toss him a grin over my shoulder while sauntering toward the stairwell. "And other times?"

"And other times ..." He climbs the stairs behind me, hands on my hips. "I want to risk getting arrested for doing inappropriate things to you in public."

I turn at the top of the stairs so we're at eye level. "Sex in public?"

His lips twitch.

"Are you a thrill seeker?" I cant my head. "Or just a run-of-the-mill sex fiend disguised as a chivalrous gentleman?"

Eric gives nothing away beyond that barely detectable smile.

"Where are you taking me tonight?"

"Concert by the river."

"Mat Kearney?"

Climbing the last two steps, he nods. I back into the door.

He might be able to control his grin, but I can't. "I love Mat Kearney."

As his hands slide along my neck, he whispers. "Lucky guy."

My next heartbeat skips, tripping my breath. Does Eric want me to love him? "I have to get ready. I don't want to be late."

"Okay." He kisses my forehead, reminding me of

his gentle side. "Wear a dress." He opens the door for me.

"Why?" I dig my key out of my bag while shuffling my feet toward my apartment.

"Easy access," he says, unlocking his door.

"Perv." I laugh.

"Only for you, Anna. Only for you."

ERIC GRINS ALL the way to the outdoor venue, clearly pleased with my sundress. We grab drinks and claim our spots while the space fills with concert-goers on this humid night.

"The braided pigtails are filling a new level of fantasies for me." He tugs on them.

"The fact that you have pigtail fantasies kinda fills a few of my fantasies." I grin.

Eric slides one arm around my waist, and his other covers my breasts, pulling my back to his chest.

I turn my head and press my lips to his bicep. "This is perfect," I murmur.

He kisses the top of my head. "It is."

Over the next two hours, I fall a little in love with Eric Steinmann while we shout lyrics into the night, sway to the ballads, and kiss between songs when the stage goes black for thirty seconds. After it's over, he takes my hand and pulls me toward the parking lot. I suck in a sharp breath when he yanks me behind a big sign surrounded by flowers.

"What are you—"

Eric's mouth covers mine in a hard kiss for several seconds before he turns me around. My hands reach for the sign to steady my shaky legs. He kisses my neck to my shoulder while he releases himself from his jeans and draws up the back of my dress.

"Eric ..." I whisper in a ragged breath.

"Shh ..." He peels my panties midway down my thighs. "Fuck ..." He groans in my ear while driving into me.

My fingers curl, nails digging into the wood sign.

I can't harness a single coherent thought. I hear the chattering crowd dispersing, the hum of cars, and squeaky breaks in the parking lot. Are we really out of sight?

I don't know.

My eyes close to focus on nothing but Eric's labored breaths at my ear, him moving inside me, and the adrenaline dripping in my veins.

"Wh-what are you doing ... to ... me?" I whisper.

He bites the skin on my shoulder. "I don't want to be the guy who gives you red roses every day."

❚❘≡❘❘❘❘≡❘❘❘❘

WE FIND a late-night burger joint and enjoy greasy food and milkshakes in a nearly empty restaurant. Eric makes me laugh until my side hurts.

"It's not funny." He pops a fry into his mouth.

I wipe tears from my eyes. "You getting locked out

of your hotel room in nothing but a towel is ..." I laugh more. "Funny. But the fact that you had to take the elevator to the lobby and..." I snort "...an elderly lady saying you should find Jesus is ..." I shake with more laughter.

Eric rolls his eyes, but he can't hide his grin. "I'm glad you find my misery so humorous."

My laughter simmers, and we spend a few seconds gazing at each other, sipping the last of our milkshakes at a quarter to midnight. This is the best feeling in the world. I don't care what we're doing. As long as I'm with Eric, life is good.

His hand slides across the table, covering mine, and I stare at our hands. "I like you." I lift my gaze to his and smile. "I like you a lot."

He nods several times. "I know the feeling all too well."

CHAPTER NINE

Book Club Night Two

I wear a pink lace cutout sundress and matching wedges to book club. Freya serves wine as everyone mills around a few minutes before seven. My heart's on the verge of bursting. I'm embarrassingly breathy while I keep my eyes glued to the door.

Where is he?

Biting the inside of my cheek, I decide it's best just to get started. He'll completely derail me once he comes through that door.

"Let's get started."

After I sit beside Freya, she hands me a generous glass of wine.

"Just in time."

I glance up at Eric taking a seat across from me. Here it comes ... the heat, the memories, the full-on blush. "Hi."

Once again, his hair is wet. I try not to focus on my intimate knowledge of him. Little things like knowing what he looks like completely naked and dripping wet in the shower. I can still feel the warm security of his embrace, those tiny moments where we know it's more than sex, but no words are necessary. The way his lips part before his tongue drags across his lower lip when I wrap my lips around his—

"They're waiting." Freya elbows me.

Shit.

When did everyone quiet down? And how long have they been staring at me, drooling over Eric while remembering the blow job I gave him last night in the shower?

"Um ..." I clear my throat and tear my gaze from Mr. Sex. "Let's start with one word that describes your feelings about chapters nine through sixteen. I'll go first. Riveting." I risk a glance at Eric, but he's focused on his plate of snacks.

The one-word descriptions follow mine: provocative, stimulating, sensual, arousing, stirring, alluring ...

My heart swells as so many accurate and positive words fall from their mouths. When it's Eric's turn, I hold my breath. I want him to be honest, but I fear his honesty could expose us to everyone. Fire fills my cheeks the second I hear his voice. With one sexual description, I could melt into a puddle.

"Eric?" Freya prompts him.

He glances up, chewing slowly, eyes wide, and gaze

shifting to me as he swallows. "Um ... do you want me to participate or just listen?"

I smile and bat my eyelashes at him. "Participate, of course."

A tiny crease forms along the bridge of his nose, and his eyes narrow a fraction. It's ... weird.

"Just say it. There's no right or wrong." Freya verbally nudges him again.

Well ... I wouldn't go so far as to say there's *no* right or wrong.

"Okay, um ..." He tips his chin and focuses on his wine glass as he swirls it. "Self-indulgent."

No one responds. Not that they need to respond. The one-word impressions don't require responses or explanations. They're just a great way to set the tone for the rest of the discussion. Or they *were* a great way to set the tone.

"Okay ... so ... what's the next question on your list?" Freya snags my book and the sticky notes with questions stuck to the cover.

"The characters are self-indulgent? Like emotionally or sexually? Or is the writing self-indulgent?" I ask.

Eric dips a baby carrot in dressing and glances up at me as he pops it into his mouth. "Uh ... is one more acceptable to you?"

My jaw drops, and I cough on my reaction between a gasp and an "uh." I'm ... dumbfounded. What is happening?

"Moving on. Do you think the accelerated pace of

Jasmine and Andrew's relationship is based on attraction or fear?" Freya reads my question.

I don't even hear the other answers. The word *self-indulgent* rings too loudly in my head. Eric won't look at me because he's a coward who just came for the free food and wine, keeping his head bowed and mouth full.

"Breathe ..." Freya whispers in my ear. "Get your shit together."

After draining my entire glass of wine, I find a smile for everyone except Eric.

I ask questions.

I share my thoughts.

I nod politely at everyone's opinions.

That's what you do in a book club.

After the final thought is shared and everyone is assigned the last third of the book for next time, I get to work on cleaning up the mess. Eric sticks around to help while keeping a safe distance. It means he's not one hundred percent stupid, but still a dick.

Even Freya remains quiet, shooting me the occasional cringe as Mr. Helpful refuses to leave.

"I'm going to take the bottles downstairs. Will you be okay?" Freya asks.

I return a slight nod while wiping down the tables.

"So just to be clear ... you want me to read the book but not have an opinion that's not the same as yours? Why didn't you just say that?"

My back straightens before I whip around to face him. "What was that last week? Were you mocking the book by doing exactly what the characters did in the book?"

"Oh, Anna ... I wasn't mocking anything." He reaches for my face, and I bat him away.

"So you just liked the scene?"

He furrows his brow. "The scene last week or the one in the book?"

"The book!"

"Well, I like what it inspired."

"Is that what you thought was self-indulgent?"

He chuckles, shaking his head. "You're quite ... spirited. I have never seen someone get so worked up over fiction. Remind me never to watch a movie with you, like blue if you like red, or choose the wrong topping on a pizza, or..." he slaps his forehead with the heel of his hand "...have an opinion that's my own."

"Why? Why play that game last week?"

Parking his hands on his hips, he lifts his gaze to the sky. "I ..." He shakes his head. "I honestly didn't think you would go there with me, and it started as a joke." He returns his attention to me. "I thought we'd laugh about it. It blew my mind that you not only latched on to my lead ... you took it. You *wanted* to be those characters."

Crossing my arms and flipping out my hip, I squint at him. "You could have stopped it."

"I wanted you any way I could get you. I'm not saying the sex scene—and what we reenacted last week —wasn't hot. It was. It was hot as fuck. *You* were hot.

Not Jasmine. Not Andrew. Who were *you* having sex with? Me? Or Andrew?"

I piece together my words without completely exposing myself. "You. I was having sex with my neighbor, Eric, whom I thought liked what he'd read ... who I thought liked my favorite book."

"I like *you*." He grabs my face before I can step back or stop him from getting a firm hold on me. "I like your passion for books. I like your passion for life. Your smile that you can't seem to hide from me. Your laughter ..." He shakes his head. "Baby, when you laugh, it's the best sound—the best feeling—in the world. You look at me like you're always two seconds away from attacking me. I like that you'd rather walk in the rain than take an Uber. I like that you shut off the shower in the middle of a blow job because you're worried about wasting water. I swear your lips were turning blue by the time I ..." he bites his lips together.

By the time he came in my mouth.

They were ... my lips were blue, and I was shivering from head to toe, but I didn't care because I wasn't distracted by wasting water, which meant I could focus on his face. I love the look he gives me when I do that to him. It's painful gratitude ... as if he loves it yet feels guilty at the same time.

Eric rests his forehead on mine. "Can we be an *us* without twenty-four chapters of something that doesn't matter?"

Life is what happens outside the bound story. Life

isn't the letters on the page; it's what inspires those words.

His words echo in my mind.

"I'm not the guy who lets you walk away. So I'll do whatever. I'll write a five-star review for your favorite book. I'll recite your favorite lines, but I won't let fiction come between us."

"Jesus ..." I whisper, tearing my face from his hands. This sucks so much. "You're nearly perfect."

He shakes his head. "I'm not, and I told you I don't want to be perfect."

I grunt a bitter laugh. "This doesn't have to be awkward. We can be neighbors, even friends. But it does have to be over." My lips pull into a sad smile. "Bye, Eric."

"Anna ... you can't be serious."

I turn and carry the last of the bags to the stairs without looking back. He's confused, and I'm embarrassed and heartbroken. It's nobody's fault. I wish that made it hurt a little less, but it doesn't.

CHAPTER TEN

"Nine out of ten people like your book choice." Freya does her best to comfort me when I feed her the "I don't want to talk about it" line for a solid week after ending things with Eric. "And one out of ten people like it when you sit on their face."

I flick a french fry at *her* face as we eat our favorite veggie burgers from the new restaurant across from the bouldering gym. "Shut up."

"Speaking of face-sitting ... Adrian will be here this weekend."

"No. Way!" I find my first genuine smile since book club. "Should we start shopping for your wedding gown?"

"I hope so, but I want to give him a chance to have second thoughts in person. I mean ... I can be a handful."

"True." I push my plate away, stuffed. "But I'm not

worried about it, and you shouldn't be either. You're a great catch."

"Thanks. Can I ask a favor?" She wipes her mouth with the napkin.

"Sure. Whatcha need?"

"I need the place to myself this weekend. I'll pay for you to stay at a hotel. A nice one with a great view."

"It's fine." I laugh. "Trust me; I don't want to be in the next room when all the sexual tension explodes. I'll stay with my parents for the night. No need to pay for a hotel room when they live fifteen minutes from here."

"You sure?"

"Positive."

"You could stay with a certain neighbor."

"Nice try. I'd stay with Carson first."

"I thought you said Carson has a new girlfriend."

I shrug. "He does."

She coughs. "You'd stay with a guy whom you have sex with on the regular when he has a girlfriend? What if she were with him?"

"It's not like I'd sleep in their bed with them. I'd stay on the couch."

"And ... that wouldn't be weird?"

"We're friends. And sometimes we have sex. We know there's a line, and we both respect that line."

"You didn't have a line with Eric?"

"Eric consumed me."

"Face-sitting. I know. Enough bragging about that."

I fling another fry at her face. "Stop it." I grin. "His confidence consumed me. It was so effortless. Things that shouldn't be sexy—not even a little bit—he made them sexy."

Like a mating dance.

"The problem was I liked him too much and cared about his opinion too much. So as trivial as disagreeing about a book probably seems to everyone else, it mattered to me. And as hard as I tried not to let it bother me, it did." I glance at my watch. "I have to get back to work."

THE FOLLOWING WEEK, Kenzie grabs my arm and pulls me into the office before I can speak. "I'm going to need more details." I pry her hand from my arm and set my purse under the desk.

"Your neighbor. The guy with the great hair?"

"Yeah?"

"He's with another girl."

"And?" I plop into the desk chair and grab the mouse, clicking on the mail inbox.

"I thought he had a thing for you. What happened? I mean, he paid me fifty dollars to make you believe he was paying a thousand for you to spot him."

"Wait ... what?"

A cringe wrinkles her face. "Sorry. It seemed like no big deal at the time."

"To lie to me?" I swivel in the chair and shoot her a look that she doesn't want if she knows what's good for her.

She shrugs. "Sorry."

"Did you give the money to the gym?"

"Um ... well ..."

"Did he pay for a day pass?"

"Oh, yeah." She sighs like that's my only concern and I won't report her to Linda. "He bought a year membership. The fifty was for me."

I narrow my eyes. We are not finished, but I have something else I need to do first. After brushing past her, I scan the gym for Eric. My gaze snags on the first shirtless guy; of course, it's him. He's watching a girl climb. As I get closer, I notice it's the employee from his shop.

Stepping behind him, I clear my throat and find a stiff smile.

He turns. "Hey."

"A word, please."

After a slight pause and narrow-eyed inspection of me, he turns back toward the wall. "Harper, I'll be right back."

I lead him to the single-stall restroom, peek inside, and nod for him to follow me when I see it's empty. I lock the door and ball my hands when the door closes behind us. "You owe this gym a thousand dollars."

It takes a few seconds for things to register, then he grins. "Nine hundred and fifty."

"A thousand. Kenzie kept your bribe, asshole. And you wasted an hour of my life."

"You look really pretty today. And I miss you." His attention drifts to my mouth.

"You know ... it's funny how you lied about paying this gym a grand for my service, but you couldn't lie about how much you detested a book."

"It's just a—"

I shake my head. "No. I'm so tired of everyone saying it's just a book. If it were *just* a book, then why not say something nice or not say anything at all? Why not show a little respect for my opinion and the opinions of other people in the group who like the book? Don't act like you're a saint for telling the 'truth' about *just a book,* then turn around and lie to spend time with me. One word ..." I hold up a finger. "You ended us with one word."

"You told me to say it."

"Not *that* word!" I rub my temples.

"Freya said there was no right or wrong answer."

"Freya lied!" Yes, I'm pissed off. I'm not mad that he doesn't like the book. I'm angry because I like him so much it's hard to focus *and* he doesn't like the book. Separately, I could deal with either thing, but not together.

Eric's brows fly up his forehead, and his head snaps backward. After several silent seconds, his shock settles into something ...

Something that makes the hair on my skin stand erect.

Something that arrests all of my thoughts.

Those piercing eyes go from wide to tiny little slits. "I think I know what you need."

"N-no ... I don't think you do. In fact—"

Fuck! NOOOOO!

He kisses me. Number one rule to breakups: NO. MORE. KISSING!

He's terrible at breaking up.

Terrible at leaving his lips off mine.

Terrible at knowing when to lie and when to tell the truth.

Eric Fucking Steinmann ...

I'm an addict, and he's an enabler. When I die of bad decisions, it will be his fault. In the meantime, I let him kiss me because I like *nearly* everything about him.

I kiss him back. God ... I love kissing him.

He shoves his hand down the front of my leggings and panties. I try to protest, but I'm already too high.

Not too high to think about his hand covered in chalk.

He's shoving his chalk fingers into my vagina!

And ... I'm letting him.

How will I explain this to my gyno guy?

So much explaining to do ...

Pissed-off Anna.

Shirtless Eric.

A kiss.

Chalk fingers in the vagina.

Painful fumbling to free one of Anna's legs from her leggings.

Eric plants Anna's bare ass on the edge of the sink.

Cock exposed.

Cock in now, chalky vagina.

Stupid. Stupid. Stupid.

The fastest orgasm record is broken.

And I'm thinking in the third person, which I do when I feel out of control—like something's not happening to me. *I* am too controlled to let something this irresponsible happen while on the clock, but that Anna girl ... has issues.

I can't let go of him. It's his labored breath and mine. My arms around his neck and my mouth pressed to his shoulder—teeth withdrawing from his skin. Eric's grip on my spread thighs eases a little, but he stays inside me. I don't want him to move. I could walk around all day with Eric's dick between my legs and never complain.

In conclusion, I, Anna Black, am a sex fiend and need help.

Holy. Fucking. Stupid! What have we done?

Eric eases out of me, steadying me with one hand while grabbing a wad of towels with his other hand.

I wrinkle my nose and take the wad from him. "Turn around."

He gives me a tense expression for a few seconds as he tucks himself back into his briefs and zips his climbing pants. Then he turns around, facing the door, while I sidestep from the sink to the toilet.

When I flush it, Eric faces me. I nod at his hands as I dry mine. He knows where those fingers have been. We stare at each other's reflection in the mirror while he washes his hands. I blow out a slow breath and wait as he dries them.

He tosses the towels into the trash. "What time do you get off work?"

"*That's* what you have to say after what just happened?" My lips part to accommodate my gasp. I'm aware of my stubbornness. The problem with stubborn people is that we are too stubborn to change even when we hear a whispered voice of reason. I have no right to be upset ... but it's happening anyway.

Eric shrugs. "Yeah. What do you want me to say? I think we covered the basics."

"We didn't cover your dick! We never cover your dick. I'd hardly say we've covered the basics. *And* you have a date waiting for you. *And* I'm supposed to be working."

That stupid smirk of his ...

"She's not my date. We just decided to climb together. The fact that she's female means nothing. And *you* dragged me in here. If you're on the clock, that's your fault, not mine. If it helps your job situation, I'll happily leave a glowing Yelp review and mention your name. The uncovered cock part was a little risky. But if I recall correctly ... we've been driving that car without brakes for weeks. We'd probably better pray on that one. But overall ... I regret nothing. Five stars all the way."

Blink.

Blink.

Blink.

Prayer? I've let myself stoop to having sex with

someone who considers prayer a form of safe sex. I need therapy.

Therapy for obsessing over a book.

Therapy for having no control over my attraction to the wrong guy.

Therapy for my flawed personality that's gotten me into this pray-the-STD-away jam I'm in.

"Listen, uh ..." I clear my throat and straighten my spine as if there's any dignity left in this tiny space after what transpired. "I think it's best if you never kiss me again." I reach past him and open the door. He hooks his finger into the waist of my leggings to stop me from leaving. Even now ... after this epic misstep in my day, there's a direct correlation between his touch and my heart rate.

"I don't have to kiss you to fuck you," he whispers in my ear before releasing me, sauntering past me, and returning to the climbing wall and his *female* buddy without another glance in my direction.

CHAPTER ELEVEN

Eric

I DON'T THINK the way to Anna's heart is through her pussy. Maybe her mouth. She seems to enjoy kissing me, but then it doesn't make much sense for her to tell me never to kiss her again. Life would be easier if I could stop thinking about her.

Stop watching her through my door's peephole.

Stop envisioning her contagious smile.

Stop loving her obsession with books, even if her taste in them is questionable.

Stop hearing her infectious laughter.

Stop craving her skin.

I do ... I *crave* her. When we kiss, I want to nibble her at the same time. My hands itch to touch her. I miss her when I go days without seeing her. My mind can't go more than five minutes—maybe five seconds— without thinking about her. Chemistry is real, and I didn't believe in it until Anna Black infiltrated my world with her witchery.

She has consumed me with no effort.

"The coffee girl?" Harper dips her hands into her chalk bag and glances past me when I return from the restroom.

"Anna. Yeah." I stare at the wall like I'm figuring out the problem.

"Her face and neck are red. She looks thoroughly flustered. You didn't ..." Harper aligns herself in front of me, attempting to snag my full attention, but she's short, so I can see over her just fine. "You didn't have sex with her in the bathroom, did you?"

Harper is my cousin Finn's girlfriend. She works part-time for me, so her curiosity runs deeper than an employee's. And Finn doesn't climb, so I'm her new best friend.

"Why would I do that?" Nope. I am not going to look at her.

"Oh, my god. You did. You totally did!"

"Shh ..." I smirk, shaking my head. "You don't know what I did or didn't do. Anna wanted to talk, so we talked."

A little. I don't remember what she first said to me because I focused too much on her lips and the probability of getting her out of those leggings without destroying them. The only words I can easily recall are the ones where she revealed her weakness.

The kiss.

She doesn't want me to kiss her because she knows that's her weakness.

"Why are you grinning like you did, in fact, have sex with her?"

I press my lips together to suppress my grin. "Did you climb that one?" I nod to the red route.

"Yes. I did that while you were having sex with Anna in the bathroom."

I have nothing but my unavoidable, truth-spilling grin.

We boulder for another hour. While we head toward the exit, I slow my pace to catch a glimpse of Anna in the office. As if she knows I'm staring at her— as if she knows she's helpless to said stare—her gaze shifts from the computer screen to me.

"I'll call you," I say with my best smile and a confident wink.

The girl who blabber-mouthed about the thousand dollars steps away from the counter to give me a better view of Anna.

"Call the gym if you have membership questions." Anna returns her gaze to the screen, nervously chewing on her bottom lip.

"My only question is, when can I kiss you again?"

Harper snorts behind me while the girl at the desk turns almost as red in the face as Anna—almost.

"I—" Anna cuts herself off, quickly glancing at Harper.

"If we need to talk privately again, the bathroom works for me." I shrug.

When Anna returns a mortified expression, Harper jerks her head toward the door. "I'm ... uh ... going to head home. See you tomorrow."

"Okay," I say without taking my eyes off Anna.

"I have a date tonight." Anna tips up her chin.

"Hmm ..." I pop my lips several times. "Why would you have a date when we just got back together?"

"We didn't get back together." She crosses her arms.

"Yeah, we did." I hold up my hands and slowly bring them together, interlacing my fingers. "We *literally* got back together."

Her face turns deep crimson while her jaw works overtime. She's not enjoying my humor. And if I'm being honest, I'm not enjoying hers. Surely this date is a joke. Right? "Lucky guy," I say, turning toward the door. "Have a good time. Make sure he pays *and* wears a condom."

Am I good with her having sex with another guy? Hell no. But fuck it all if I'm going to let her see my disappointment.

I don't miss her tiny flinch as she deflates a fraction, which feels like a win for me or at least a point.

"Later, neighbor."

CHAPTER TWELVE

Anna

"So you ARE a thing." Kenzie eyes me after the door closes behind Eric.

"No." I return to the office, keeping my gaze on my feet, my heart locked in self-preservation, and my mind replaying his words.

Eric swooped into my life and claimed way more headspace than I could afford to give him. I wish I knew how to take it back. Erase all that we've done.

I wish I could unmeet him and have a redo under different circumstances.

After work, I take my computer to Ritual Cafe, where I have a date with a brownie, a cup of decaf, and my laptop to get more work done. An hour after pushing myself to focus, I dig my Kindle out of my handbag and bring up *The Last Person*.

I reread one page at a time, one line at a time. Maybe Eric's right.

Maybe it's a flawed story.

Maybe the writing is sophomoric.

Maybe it's *redundant, predictable,* and *self-indulgent.*

Maybe B. Ashton will never write another book.

Maybe I'm not only her number one fan but her *only* fan.

It's just ...

It's tough to fall in love with something and feel judged for that love. Books possess power. They are no more ink and paper than humans are flesh and bones.

Humans have souls ... books have souls.

They reach across oceans. Bridge divides.

They are so much more than the hands that write them. Books transcend time. Stories don't die. They are immortal. They are timeless.

I guess I'm a romantic for books. When someone shares my love of a story, it reaches deeper than a kiss, and it's a bond that can't be broken.

That's why I should only let Eric steal me momentarily, give him my flesh and bones and my temporary wandering mind. What happens when the physical fades, and we're left with the hard reality that his wind doesn't blow in the direction of my soul?

I chuckle at the *direction* of my mind.

"Laughing at yourself?"

My head jerks toward the familiar voice.

"Hey, Carson. What are you up to?" I move my bag so he can take a seat.

"Saw you in the window."

"Laughing at myself?" I wrinkle my nose.

"Yeah." He slides his leg against mine.

My eyebrows lift. "How's the new girlfriend?"

"She got a job offer in Minneapolis and took it."

I sip my second cup of coffee, that's now lukewarm.

"You seeing anyone?"

My gaze follows my cup as I set it on the table. "Can I tell you something?"

"Of course." He runs his hand through his thick, blond hair before leaning back in his chair and crossing his arms.

"I've been seeing this guy off and on. I like him, and he's fun."

"That's code for he's good in bed?" One of Carson's eyebrows peaks. He knows.

Biting my lower lip, I nod.

He nudges my leg. "How good?"

"Jealous?"

He twists his lips. "Should I be?"

I shut my laptop and rest my head on my hands. "I don't know. I'm not sure it's some God-given gift. It's pheromones. Chemistry. Something more than memorizing the playbook. It's not better." Lifting my head, I shake it. "Or maybe it is. I'm not sure. It's just different. We almost fit. And that's *almost* a great feeling."

Carson chuckles. "Almost? Isn't close enough good enough?"

"Close is worse than completely being the wrong fit. It's like the puzzle piece that almost fits. You try it a hundred different ways because it's so damn close, and you want it to be the right piece."

"So what's the snag? Why is he not the perfect fit?"

Grunting a quick laugh, I gaze over Carson's shoulder because I can't tell him the truth and look him in the eye. "He doesn't like my favorite book."

Silence.

After a good ten seconds, I risk direct eye contact.

"I'm sorry. Did you say he doesn't like your favorite book?"

I knew he'd react this way, but I still frown like I expected a different reaction. "If a girl you liked didn't like your dog, it would be a dealbreaker, and you know it."

He sits up straight, withdrawing his leg from its spot next to mine. "Yo ... you know my *dog's* name is Gilbert, and you can't compare a dog to a book. Sorry. Nice try. Now tell Mr. Almost Perfect that you screwed up and let a book get in the way."

"I love Gilbert, and you know it, but I don't love you at the moment, even if we're forever friends with benefits. Just because you don't read anything that's not a blog doesn't make books anything short of the perfect soulmate."

"Whoa ... maybe I need to read this soulmate book."

"No. You don't. If you don't love it, we'll be over. If

you do love it, you'll have to marry me. And if I'm being frank, I have a slight dog allergy."

"Seriously?" He cocks his head to the side.

My nose scrunches. "Seriously. I love him but I always leave with an itchy throat, watery eyes, and some phlegm."

"You're right. I can't read the book and risk having to marry you. If I have to choose, I'll choose Gilbert."

I smile. "If I were in your shoes, I'd choose him too. Allergies aren't sexy, and I won't lick your legs after you get back from jogging. I know that's important to you."

"So ... maybe we save you from phlegm and just go to your place tonight if you have no intention of choosing Mr. Almost Perfect over your hardbound soulmate."

I slide my laptop into my bag. "My copy is a paperback."

"That's unfortunate." Carson has a special kind of sarcasm that makes it impossible to keep a straight face.

"It really is." I sling my bag over my shoulder and head toward the door.

Carson slides past me to open it. "Did you bike?"

"You betcha." I nod toward the black horseshoe-shaped beam with my bike locked to it.

"I can give you a ride home, and we can get your bike in the morning."

"It's supposed to rain. And I'm uncomfortable leaving my new bike here all night. That lock isn't top-notch."

"I'll drive slowly then." He unlocks his car while I open my chain.

"The race is on." I wink and take off before he gets into his silver Mercedes. I don't intend to sleep with him, but I need the comfort of something or someone besides my wandering thoughts.

Despite crawling through the streets of downtown and intentionally hitting all the red lights, he still beats me to my apartment. I push my bike past him as if I don't see him leaning against the maple tree with one leg crossed over the other, looking quite casual.

"Who's letting Gilbert out?" I ask as if I'm talking to the wind, looking straight ahead at the door.

Carson pushes off the tree and follows me. "My neighbor."

"The one you slept with?"

"You'll have to be more specific." He opens the door after I swipe my card over the reader.

"Such a manwhore."

"Yet, here you are ... taking me to your place for the night."

"Not to have sex." I lock up my bike and head up the stairs.

"Whoa. Whoa. Whoa ..." He grabs my hand to stop me.

I let him yank me toward him just before the stairway door. "Whoa, what?"

He frowns. "I'm not here to cuddle."

"I can't have sex with you."

He laughs, sliding his arms around my waist. "And

why not? Is it that time of the month? I'm good with shower sex."

Nibbling at the corner of my bottom lip, I shake my head.

"No? Then what?" He cants his head.

"I'd rather not say." I escape his embrace and head toward my apartment.

"Vague is not your MO. What's going on?"

Before I can answer, Eric's door opens. He fills the space with his shirtless torso and his usual sexy jeans—freshly showered hair. It's weird that a guy who owns a T-shirt shop wears one so infrequently. Was he watching for me?

"Hey." My mouth tries to find a casual smile where my lips don't quiver as much as my voice—total fail.

"Hi." Eric's gaze goes straight to Carson.

"Sorry ... uh ... Eric, Carson. Carson, Eric."

No handshakes are swapped, just two men sizing each other up as if they know I've had sex with the other one.

"You staying?"

Wow. Just ... wow. Have to hand it to Eric; he wastes no time getting to the point.

"Why should you care?" Carson rests his hand on the small of my back.

Eric ignores the possessive move on Carson's part, keeping his gaze locked on mine. "We had sex in the bathroom of the bouldering gym earlier today. No condom. I'm just saying ... proceed with caution. You don't know where my dick has been. Have a good night." He takes a step back.

After a final ruling, the door shuts like a gavel: my life sucks.

Kill me now.

Carson steps in front of me, forcing me to acknowledge him—to answer the question before he asks it. I don't need to answer it. The truth blooms in my cheeks and wrinkles my face as a permanent cringe.

"*Now* I know why we're not having sex tonight." He shakes his head before rolling his eyes to the ceiling. A long, heavy breath shoots out his nose as he bites his lips together.

"I ..." I rub my temples. "I can't believe he just said that."

"Well ..." Carson grunts, returning his attention to me. "It's the right thing to say when you don't want another guy fucking your girl."

"I'm not his girl."

Biting the inside of his cheek while studying me for a few seconds, he shakes his head slowly. "I've known you for years. We've had sex countless times. I know you're on the pill, and you know I get tested regularly. Yet ... you've never even considered letting me stick my dick in you without a condom." Bending forward, he kisses my cheek and slides his mouth to my ear. "You're definitely his girl," he whispers. His declaration makes the hair along my neck stand up and my pulse surge.

My defenses send my thoughts into a frenzy. I'm not Eric's anything. I'm just ... I'm ...

Closing my eyes because I don't know what I am, I wait to no longer feel Carson's touch. I wait for his steps to fade, the door to the stairway to shut, and for my anger to find the correct target.

My hands curl into fists, desperate to bang down Eric's door. All these words no longer want to be muted, suppressed, and ignored. My insecurities win, guiding me to my door instead of his. As I open my door, I hear the faintest noise behind me.

It's him. I don't have to turn around. I just know.

"I like you. A lot."

I nod slowly. "That's a relief. I'd be pissed off if you felt the need to trample my evening by confessing intimate details without *really* liking me first." I turn.

"What must I do to make you not want to bring other guys home? Flowers with the petals still on the stems?"

I tell my lips to remain neutral. He hasn't earned a grin, but damn ... it's hard. The problem is that I like him too—a lot.

"A journal of all my thoughts about you in a day?" he asks.

That one hits me in the feels.

"A night of cuddling instead of sex?"

My gaze drops to the floor between us.

"Old school? Need I remind you that I formally asked you to be my girlfriend?"

I slowly shake my head.

"If I kiss you again, will you push me away?"

"Don't kiss me," I whisper, feeling ...

Feelings ...

I have these crazy strong feelings for him. I'm attracted to him and angry at him ... even when I'm clawing at his skin, desperate to feel him inside me. It's so messed up. Attraction like this is a drug that plays havoc with every ounce of sensibility I have left in my brain.

"What will you do if I kiss you?" He steps closer, putting us toe to toe where I can smell that heady mix of spice and citrus and feel the heat from his bare chest.

"I'd kiss you back," I say just above a whisper. "And I wouldn't be able to stop. I'm *asking* you not to kiss me. If I get lost in you, I will lose myself."

"And that's bad?" He lifts my chin with his finger.

"It would be tragic."

He studies me through narrowed eyes for a few seconds before dropping his finger from my chin and shaking his head. "I don't understand. If it's just sex, I'm way off because it feels like more than sex."

"What if it's not? What if I like how you fuck me, and that's where it ends?"

I hate that he flinches. And I hate how it sounds because I don't mean it.

"Then I'll take you any way I can get you."

Before I can react or show the slightest sign of refusing him, he kisses me, and I don't even fight it. We kiss. Anyone can see us from their peephole, an open door, or walking up the stairway. By the time he carries me to his doorway, my shirt hangs around my neck, and he palms my ass with one hand and shoves my bra up over my breasts with his other hand.

Drugs. Only drugs make people this stupid. I need to check into rehab ... after one ... more ... hit.

What's the best way to redeem oneself after reckless, unprotected sex? More reckless, unprotected sex. He's deep inside me within seconds of the door closing behind us, and we make it no farther than the sofa.

Clothes half on, half off.

"I'm not sharing you," he whispers in my ear, a breath before biting the skin along my neck.

I have no desire to be shared. His body moves above mine on the sofa. One of his hands pins both of mine above my head while he drives into me repeatedly. It's sexy. *He's* sexy.

My head lulls to the side as I fight back my orgasm. I don't want this to end. Eric is *the* guy.

And then it happens ... my gaze focuses on the pile of books atop his coffee table. *The Last Person* is at the bottom.

I'm at the bottom.

We're both getting fucked by this man. And I hate that my mind goes there. If I could make it stop, I would. So I close my eyes and focus on him inside of me. It feels good. He smells good and tastes good. Everything is good.

But it's not!

The. Fucking. Book.

Either books are ruining me for men, or men are

ruining me for books. Well, just one man ... and one book.

"I ... I can't." I wriggle.

"What?" he asks with a strained voice as he speeds up his motions, sweat beading along his forehead.

"I said I can't!" I push at his chest again.

Eric stops and pulls out of me. I fall to the floor and shoot to my feet, piecing myself back together.

"Did I hurt you?" Confusion lines his face as he slides up his briefs and jeans while lifting his pelvis from the sofa.

Yes. He hurt me, just not the way he thinks he did. I don't look at him. My gaze stays on the book as I thread my arms through my shirt. The human brain is terrible. Thoughts are the worst poison. I'm fucking toxic to myself, and I can't stop it.

Eric's gaze tracks mine. "Please tell me this isn't about the stupid book." His fingers thread into his hair.

It sucks to be in the "it's not you, it's me" rut. Yet, here I am.

⁕ ⁕ ⁕

"WANT TO TALK ABOUT IT?" Mom asks after I invite myself to dinner for the third night in a row.

After storming out of Eric's place, the last thing I need is to run into him. I'm sure he's bewildered. One minute we're having great sex, and the next minute I'm shoving him away, throwing on my clothes, and running out the door with nothing more than an "it's over."

"I'm having issues with this guy I like." Squinting against the sun, I sip my glass of wine while we watch Dad turn the chicken on the grill.

Like is the wrong word. On the one hand, my feelings have reached beyond "like," but on the other hand, he feels like the bane of my existence. I *like* having sex with him, and I more than *like* being in his arms or the adoration I feel from him when he does nothing more than smile at me. He's friendly ... says hi to everyone, whether he knows them or not. He likes to read. It's not that he doesn't have potential. He does. Just not with me because I'm an incurable, self-destructive, fucked-up bibliophile.

"What issues?"

"Just different tastes in things."

"He's not a climber?"

"Ha! No. That's not it. He climbs, and he's outstanding. A phenomenal climber. It's his taste in literature."

"Literature?"

Gah! It sounds ridiculous, but it's not. "He joined our book club. We're reading my pick ... my favorite book. And he doesn't like it *at all*."

Incredulity lines Mom's face. "A book?"

"He called it redundant, repetitive, and sophomoric."

"Is it?"

"What?" I flinch. "No. Of course not." I rub my

temples and shake my head. "How can I make you understand? It's like …. you love your rose bushes. What if Dad hated them and—"

"I do hate them," Dad says.

"Not helping, Dad." I roll my eyes. "Fine. He doesn't like them, but he trims them, feeds them, and is careful not to harm them when he mows the lawn and uses the weed eater. What if he trampled them and called them ugly weeds? What if he said anyone who likes roses is stupid? How would that make you feel?"

Mom's body bounces while she chuckles. "Oh, dear. Did this guy you like call you stupid for liking the book you chose?"

"Well, no. But by degrading the book and the writing, it was implied."

"Or just a difference of opinion." Dad shrugs, closing the lid on the grill. "I love mushrooms, and your mom hates them."

"Not the same thing." I frown. "When you love a story, it resonates in some way with your heart or maybe even your soul."

"What's the title of this book? Maybe I need to read it?"

I smile at my mom. "I have my copy in my bag, and you really should read it."

"But for the love of god … if you don't like it, keep that shit to yourself." Dad thinks he's funny.

He's not.

CHAPTER THIRTEEN

Eric

Anna left.

I didn't chase her.

If we can't be ninety-nine percent amazing together and let that other one percent (the book) fade into the background, I'm fighting a losing battle. After all, I can't turn back time and pretend I love something I don't. When I asked her never to surrender, I didn't anticipate her taking it so literally.

"Hey! What's up?" I answer my phone, seeing my dad's picture pop up onto the screen.

"Can you thin my slush pile?"

I laugh. "Do I have to?"

"Yes. I already sent five. They'll arrive later today, and I sent them to your store so you can sign for them."

"And how long do I have?"

"A week."

I shake my head, standing from my desk as the front door to the store rings from someone opening it. "Just fantastic. About a book a day."

"You didn't have other plans anyway. Right?"

"No, Dad. No plans. Gotta go."

Two hours later, the package arrives, and I grab dinner on the way home.

As soon as I open the apartment building's door, Anna glances up from the bike rack. Two other residents are in the entry, so I don't feel obligated to acknowledge her. She didn't want to sleep with anyone in the building because things could be awkward.

Well, here I am ... smiling at everyone, including her. Same smile. Nothing special. I'm not making anything awkward as I carry my package and dinner past her. She tips her chin down and slips off her helmet.

That's right ... you should hide your face in shame. You crazy book lady.

She kicked and shoved me like a toddler having a tantrum. I didn't appreciate her making me feel like I was forcing myself on her. I wasn't.

After I get my dinner set out on my table, I open the package of manuscripts. The slush pile of unsolicited crap—at least ninety-nine out of a hundred is complete garbage. Occasionally, there's a hidden gem. Dad's looking for that *one* and must feel indifferent about other clients' work. My parents have owned a publishing company for twenty years, and I'm expected to take over when they retire. In the meantime, they use me for fun stuff like the slush pile. My head already aches, and I haven't even started.

All five manuscripts have tags on them. They're the ones my mom peeked at and didn't hate the first three chapters.

I thumb through them, deciding which will ruin my night the least.

Elenor's Boyfriend

Hard pass.

Waking Up In His Arms

Hell no.

Journey to The Missing Planet

It's a possibility. I'd rather go to the missing planet than meet Elenor's boyfriend or wake up in some guy's arms.

Sex on Medicare

What the fuck? I remind myself that my mom read at least a few chapters and saw something. She might need to get new glasses.

The Last Person

I chuckle. Great. Another book with that title, and sadly, it's probably better than Anna's obsession. My gaze slides an inch lower to the author—B. Ashton.

Fuck. My. Life.

Really? How did Anna pick an indie book submitted to my parents' publishing house? I envision myself recommending this be the one they publish. B. Ashton gets her book in bookstores and airport gift shops. I take Anna to the locally owned bookstore on the corner and show her the colossal display of *The*

Last Person in the window. Then I tell her it was because of me. I made it happen. She takes me back to her place. We fuck like rabbits. The End.

I laugh out loud. Yeah ... that's not happening. If I run out of toilet paper, I might use pages of the manuscript to wipe my ass, but that's the most appreciation this book will get from me.

Truth? I didn't initially hate it. I just didn't see a wow factor. The writing is good, and there's potential. But after weeks and weeks of it cockblocking me, I detest it.

"Looks like I'm taking a journey to the missing planet." I push the manuscripts aside and slide my plate in front of me. As I try to enjoy my dinner, the stupid manuscript haunts me.

How does this happen? Millions of books. Millions of manuscripts. And *this* one lands in my lap.

I grab a red pen and start marking up *The Last Person*. My dad only wants my opinion. He's not expecting me to return an edited manuscript, but I must do this. I need to get it out of my system ... the book out of my system ... *her* out of my system.

By five the following morning, with no sleep for my wary body, and pages of red marks and long notes, I turn to the last page. The words wait for me to swallow them, to make sense of them as I read a copy of the query letter.

I can't. They lodge into my chest, making it hard to breathe. I feel ... No. There are no words to describe how I feel.

Anger.

Confusion.

Disbelief.

Resentment.

All good words, but not the right ones.

Dragging my exhausted ass into the bathroom, I shower and go to work. It takes four espressos to get through the day. By the time I get home, I'm ready to collapse.

"Going to the next book club?" Piper asks when she starts up the stairs behind me.

I stop midway to the second floor and glance over my shoulder. "That's tonight?"

She nods and smiles. "Yes. We're finishing the discussion tonight. That ending! Did you finish it?"

Even the muscles in my face are too exhausted to pull into a readable expression. I nod. "Did you like the story?"

"Loved it!" She passes me, clicking her heels on the stairs to the third floor.

"Can I ask how many books you read in a year?" I yell up to her.

"Twenty to thirty." She stops and peeks her head over the railing. "Why?"

Chewing the inside of my cheek, I shake my head. "No reason."

"Did you not like it?"

I continue shaking my head while my feet drag my ass the rest of the way to the second floor. "Doesn't matter," I mumble.

Setting the alarm on my phone, I give myself an hour of sleep to take the edge off so I can start another manuscript before bedtime. When I wake up, I stare at the time. It's thirty minutes until book club ... until Anna's friends praise her for her excellent book pick. There's a one hundred percent chance she doesn't want me there.

If my brain was working correctly, with more than an hour's sleep in the past day, I'd eat, read, and go to sleep without giving that woman or her favorite book a second thought. Sadly, it's not working right. So I change my clothes, grab my paperback copy of the book, and head to the rooftop.

When I push through the heavy door, Anna's gaze finds me in less than two seconds, her sad eyes narrowing a fraction. I give her nothing because I don't know exactly how I feel. The right words still don't exist.

"Oh, hey, Eric." Freya offers me a stiff smile.

"Hi." I nod.

"This is my fiancé, Adrian." She tugs on the short, dark-haired kid's arm. Yes ... he looks maybe sixteen, but I'm sure he's of legal age.

"Hi." It's my best, non-confrontational greeting. I'm not here to bring trouble. Not yet, anyway.

He returns a similar nod of acknowledgment.

"Everyone take a seat," Anna beckons the chattering members to the sofas.

My ass plants itself at the far end.

"Okay. Let's go around and give our one-word

impression of the ending." Anna's eyes lift from her book, her gaze sweeping to everyone but me.

"Unexpected."

"Shocking."

"Perfection."

"Satisfying."

Everyone shares their words. Anna's posture builds into a statue of pride with each passing second.

"Eric, your turn." Ashlee nudges my arm.

I stare at the book on my lap. "Ambiguous."

"Huh ... so you felt the ending was open to interpretation?" Freya asks.

I shrug, keeping my head down. "Something like that," I murmur.

"Well, anyway ..." Anna jumps in and starts a specific topic of conversation.

I let my gaze find her, and I don't look away—not when she risks a glance at me, laughs, or sips her wine and nods in agreement with the discussion. I watch her and wonder why.

After it's over and everyone starts to make their way toward the exit, I don't move.

"We'll give you a few minutes," Freya says to Anna before she and her fiancé exit the rooftop leaving just the two of us.

Anna tries to ignore me, picking up trash and gathering the wine bottles.

I watch her.

She lowers the umbrellas and sets the trash bag by the door.

I watch her.

"Why are you here?" She parks in front of me, arms crossed. I don't get an angry vibe from her. It's a sad one.

I toss my book, along with a Sharpie, onto the table beside me. "Thought I'd ask B. Ashton to sign my book."

"W-what are you talking about?"

"You know exactly what I'm talking about," I grunt, resting my elbows on my knees and running my hands through my hair.

"How?" she whispers.

"Roseland Publishing. Roseland was my grandmother—a poet. My parents named their publishing company after her. My dad sent me some manuscripts from his slush pile to read through. Can you guess whose manuscript was in that pile?" I lift my gaze. "With a copy of the query letter and the author's real name?"

Her eyes turn red with unharnessed emotion.

"Why?"

She slowly shakes her head. "I was afraid."

"If you're afraid, you don't pick your own damn book for the book club. You had to have a certain level of confidence to do that."

She continues to shake her head. "I wanted honest feedback, more than just a review online. But I didn't want anyone to feel obligated to say nice things because they knew it was my book."

"Bullshit!" I stand, forcing her to take a few steps

backward.

She flinches.

"If you wanted honest feedback, you would have asked *me* for more of my thoughts on the book. You wanted your ego stroked, and when I refused to comply, you acted like a fucking child."

"Screw you."

"You did. You screwed me. Only I didn't realize we were a threesome. Had I known beforehand, I might have slipped on my kid gloves and been slightly less honest. That's what you wanted. Right? Sugar-coated honesty? Did you want to know about the two hundred and thirty-seven typos that your editor missed before you self-published? Did you want to know that your timeline is off? Or is that too much too? Because I can guarantee you that a publisher will not hold back. They will tell you exactly what needs to be changed to improve your story. They'll probably take out all the parts that you love the most. They'll ask you to rewrite entire chapters and frown upon your excessive use of passive tense. They'll make judgments on your characters and suggest you do something to lessen the extreme bitchiness of your heroine. And you'll get your back up because you know that deep down, that heroine is you."

She tips her chin up. "The reviews online are excellent."

I shake my head. "I looked—two-hundred reviews. Let's talk about reviews when you have two thousand. Or more like twenty thousand, which will give us a better idea of what a hundred thousand might look like if you get published. For all we know, you have two hundred loyal friends right now."

"None of my friends know it's my book!"

"It doesn't matter."

"You hate it, so you assume everyone else will hate it. Well, you're wrong."

"I never said I hated it."

She flips her hip out and crosses her arms. "So you're going to publish it?"

"No." I chuckle. "You self-published, and you tested a small market. Good for you. The fact that you self-published at all makes you a little less appealing to publishers. Write another book and keep building your audience. Or write another book and submit it before you publish it."

"But I already wrote a book. And I don't care what you think ... I left my soul in that book. I worked my ass off to write that book, and that could be my best work."

"Well," I shrug, "then I suggest you keep your day job. Good luck." I brush past her toward the door.

"You're an asshole."

"Okay." I don't glance back at her.

"I'll just send it to more publishers and agents. I'm not giving up."

"Okay." I keep walking.

"And you're going to feel like such a fool when this is a bestseller, and you passed it up."

"We'll see about that." I open the door and leave her behind with her gigantic ego.

CHAPTER FOURTEEN

Anna

THE NEXT FEW days are a blur. I need to move past this. I need to move past him. However, I don't need to hear Freya's sex chants the second I open the apartment door. I gave them plenty of time alone to work that shit out, but she has no self-control. Dare I knock on the door and ask Adrian to shove a pillow over her face?

Thank you, God.

Her bedroom door opens, so I stay hidden in the kitchen. Last night I got to see all of Adrian, which I never want to see again.

Little man. Big dick. It's too weird.

"Anna?"

Thankfully it's Freya. I close the fridge and face her robe-wrapped body, red hair a mess.

"Yes?"

Her nose wrinkles. "Do you ..."

"Do I?"

"Have any lube?"

I blink several times.

"We wanna try something."

"It won't fit." I cringe. Those words come out of total instinct. "I mean ... no, I don't have lube. Freya, just go to sleep. Don't you have to work tomorrow?"

She rolls her eyes and walks toward me. "Yes, but it's only nine-thirty. I wonder if something like olive oil would work."

"Whoa!" I snatch the bottle by the stove before she grabs it. "No. I bought this. I don't mind you using it for cooking, but I'm not letting you take it into the bedroom."

"I'll buy you a new bottle."

I continue to hug the olive oil to my chest. "What if it's not safe? What if it reacts with the latex condom and weakens it?"

Her brow furrows. "You think we should use a condom? We've both been tested, and we're done with ...." She rubs her lips together and somewhat indiscreetly points her finger south. "The front hole."

Shoving the bottle toward her, I grimace. "Take it; just stop talking about it. And you owe me a new bottle. Same brand, and no cheap shit."

"Thanks, Anna. You're the best!" She scurries off with the bottle.

Within minutes, the apartment is filled with a new chant—oh ... ow ... god ... slower.

Thankfully, I don't have to work tomorrow. Snatching my purse from the counter, I head to the bar across the street next to the pizza place where I had my first official date with the jackass neighbor guy.

"Anna Black, what can I get you?" Travis asks me from behind the bar as he flips a white towel over his shoulder.

"Let's see ... Freya just took my expensive bottle of olive oil to her bedroom to use as lube ..." I tap my finger on my chin.

Travis laughs. "Tequila it is."

After two shots, I forget about my olive oil, and my relaxed gaze starts to wander around the bar, snagging on the couple toward the back by the restrooms.

Eric Fucking Steinmann has a beer in one hand and the ass of some girl in his other hand while they stand in a circle chatting with another couple I've never seen before.

When Eric's attention shifts to the television for a few seconds and then makes its casual sweep of the room, I can't avert my gaze fast enough. And once he notices me, I find moving any part of my body impossible.

I hate him.

He's pure evil.

If the devil walked the earth in human form, it would be Eric Steinmann, looking like sin, fucking women in public restrooms, and eyeing them in bars like he's doing to me.

He's right. I should write another book. He'll be

the villain, and the heroine will kill him, but not before removing his balls with toenail clippers and his dick with a nail file.

I have a mani-pedi tomorrow ... they're the first weapons that come to mind.

My phone chimes, bringing me out of my murderous trance. It's a text from my mom.

> I just finished The Last Person. It was okay. Don't be mad. I'm not sure it's the best book I've ever read. Some areas of the story were a bit wordy, and I'm surprised I found so many typos in a published book. Sidenote: Did you see the new miniseries released on Hulu? Good night.

My heart sinks into the pit of my stomach. There it is. The person who should be the most biased about me and my writing is my mom. And she would be ... if she knew I wrote the book.

She doesn't. I never told anyone because I didn't want to see their faces if I failed. This makes my mom the most authentic example of unbiased honesty—the best constructive criticism and a reality check I didn't see coming.

I take down another shot of tequila ... then another. Then I have to pee. Luckily, I have just enough alcohol in my body not to care that Eric and his new girl are blocking the way to the toilet.

Swaying a bit as I stand, I gather my bearings and worm through the crowd, feeling slightly numb while the room spins. "Excuse me. Pardon me," I mumble. As I approach Eric, he eyes me with a worried brow and pitiful frown.

"Excuse me. I need through to pee." I offer a stiff grin.

The blond girl on his arm and the other couple smile and part the sea for me to pee. I giggle when I realize my brain rhymed. Maybe I'm not a novelist. Perhaps I'm a poet like Eric's grandma.

I take a few wobbly steps, and Eric's hand moves from the blond girl's ass to my arm, steadying me.

"Anna, I think you should go home," he says.

My hands fly out to the side like a cat preparing to land on its feet. "I'm good. I just need to pee and can't go home until anal is over." I continue forward as Eric's friends snigger behind me.

"You know her?" One of them asks.

"Sort of. Just a sec," he replies as I reach for the door handle.

"That's the men's room." His hand covers mine, peeling my grip from the handle and redirecting me to the next door, a few more feet down the hallway.

It's locked.

I sigh, rolling to the side, pressing my back against the wall, and closing my eyes so things stop moving on me. "You 'sort of' know me? Well, that's just fantastic. Go," I mumble. "Blond girl's ass is probably missing your hand. Can't blame her ... I remember what that feels like."

"You're drunk, and I didn't have my hand on her

ass. It's called her lower back. What are you doing here by yourself getting wasted?"

I rub my temples. "My mom didn't love the book. Freya has a dick up her ass, and she's being loud about it. And my chances of finding a publisher are nearly zero, so I think I deserve a few shots."

Eric glances down the hallway to his friends. "Can you get home by yourself?"

The door to the bathroom opens. The woman coming out gives us a quick smile and turns the corner.

I laugh. "You have a date, and I have to pee."

He shrugs. "It's not a date. I just met her here. I ... we ..."

I rest my hand on his chest. "You..." my head tries to spin again "...will sleep with her. She's not a psycho-author. She seems like a good distraction. I get it." I turn and flip on the light to the bathroom. "I used to be a good distraction until you ruined it." Closing the door, I lock it and find the toilet before I wet my pants.

When I emerge, he's gone. His friends are gone. And I'm oddly disappointed. It has to be the tequila.

I take my inebriated self home. The apartment is quiet. After erasing my mom's text without responding, I resist my usual urge to jump online and check my book sales. I wouldn't call four copies a day something that will pay the rent. Tequila, Mom, and Eric mix into a potent cocktail of self-doubt. I decide to face the truth.

I'm not a writer.

The following day, I awaken with a nasty hangover

but a new lease on life. I'm not a writer, and this means I can figure out what I am good at. For now, it's marketing at the bouldering gym.

"Morning," Finn says as I arrive for my morning java.

"Good morning."

"Usual?"

I nod.

"So I heard you're an author."

I peer up from my phone. "Um ..."

He nods behind me. I glance over my shoulder to Eric sitting at a table with his coffee and a stack of papers.

He smiles, much like he did the day we met.

I turn back to Finn. "I'm not." How nice of Eric to blab it to everyone, and I can only imagine what he said about my subpar abilities to pen something worthy of a spot on someone's bookshelf.

Grabbing my coffee, I march toward the door, keeping my gaze away from Eric.

"Do you want it?" His voice stops me.

"Want what?" I ask, both words lined with exasperation.

"Your manuscript."

I glance to the side as he digs into his messenger bag, pulls out another pile of papers, and plops them on the table.

I squint at it while inching a little closer. "I didn't send a physical copy."

"They print it. I'm old school like my parents, and I like to make physical notes the first time through."

I pick it up, the slew of red marks from the second page bleeding through to the title page. "Did you edit it? Why edit something you don't intend to publish?"

"As a favor to you."

"How kind. Maybe you'll also critique the cellulite on my legs and my small boobs as *a favor*."

"I haven't noticed your cellulite, and your boobs are fine. What is it they say ... anything more than a mouthful is a waste?"

"You're a dick." I hug the manuscript to my chest and bring my coffee to my mouth with my other hand.

"Maybe." He shrugs. "Just so you know..." he nods to the manuscript, "...I wasn't in a good place when I made the edits, which means I mentioned every little thing and used many exclamation points in my notes, which was very unprofessional. My bad."

My bad?

How did I let myself get entangled with this guy?

Dropping the manuscript on top of the other manuscript in front of him, my lips pull into a firm line, and I set my coffee down before removing the lid to his large coffee and dumping it all over both manuscripts.

Eric jerks back in his chair, attempting to avoid it spilling onto his lap. "What the hell?"

"Sorry. My bad." I grab my coffee, pivot, and don't look back.

"Get your stubborn ass back here!" He grabs his

bag and gathers the wet manuscripts, depositing them in the garbage as he follows me out the door.

I lengthen my strides. "Screw you, Eric Steinmann!"

"You did! That's just it. And it was so goddamn unforgettable that I felt angry that you lied to me, that you let a book ruin it. So I took it out on your manuscript." He grabs my shoulder and forces me to stop, placing himself in front of me like an angry roadblock.

"Oh, gosh ... I'm so sorry. I'm sure the blond girl from last night can spread her legs just as wide as I can spread mine. So save 'the sex was goddamn unforgettable' story for someone else."

"It was more than the sex, and you know it." He steals my coffee and struts in the other direction.

"Hey!" I chase him.

Fishing a key from his pocket, he opens the door to his T-shirt shop. I reach for the handle before it shuts.

He pivots and glares at me, but I don't flinch. He's done making me feel bad about myself and intimidating me. Reaching past me, he locks the door and takes *my* coffee to his office.

"If it were more than sex, you would not have made me feel bad about myself."

He sets the coffee on the desk and looks up at me with total disbelief. "I DIDN'T KNOW IT WAS YOUR BOOK!"

I jump, heart racing.

He blows out a long breath, the expression on his red face softening into regret. "I didn't know ..."

"What would you have done ... had you known?" I whisper.

He shakes his head. "I don't know. I ... I would have lied. And maybe it wouldn't have felt like a total lie, and maybe I wouldn't have been able to read it through clear glasses. A blinding desire."

"I'm done. I will pull the book from retailers, and I'm just ... done."

Eric's forehead wrinkles, and he nods slowly.

"That's it?" I cough for a second in disbelief. "A nod? Are you not going to tell me not to give up? To write another book?"

He eases into his chair and folds his hands over his red T-shirt-clad chest. "Successful people have one thing in common—they're self-motivated. If I have to tell you not to give up, to write another book, and fight for your dreams ... you'll never be a published author. Period."

I thought my world was crumbling when he told me his parents owned Roseland Publishing and he had my manuscript. I felt the same when my mom texted me with her lukewarm opinion of my book.

I was wrong.

Right now ... I feel like a massive failure because part of me needs outside approval, a pat on the back, and words of encouragement. *This* is my lowest point.

Picking up my knocked-out ego, I slide it into my pocket and smile at Eric while I close the distance between us with hesitant steps. He sits up straight, spreading his knees wide to accommodate my body to stand between them. My hands press to his cheeks, and he leans into my touch. It makes things so much harder, but I do it anyway. I love him. I will never say those words, but I love him. Despite *everything* ... I love him.

But I'm broken.

I'm lost.

I'm hurt.

My lips press to his in a slow kiss. His initial hesitation tells me he's not expecting this. Not now. Maybe not ever again. Pulling back, I hold his gaze, admiring the wonder in his eyes. He's trying to figure out what's happening, what it means.

"Thank you," I whisper.

Snagging my coffee from his desk, I leave his store and his life.

CHAPTER FIFTEEN

Three years later ...

Eric

WHEN I GROW UP, I want to be a ...

Hell, I still don't know. After giving *the girl* a speech on following dreams and achieving success and then letting her walk out of my life, I've managed to jump from T-shirts to publishing to journalism. My parents sold their publishing company, which prompted me to write an article on a monetized blogging platform about big publishers gobbling up smaller publishers and the effect on the world. That's led to several contributing editor positions with major online news outlets.

Then my mom decided to leave my dad.

My dad decided to stop showering, shaving, or caring about life.

Now we're roommates.

"How do you feel about an exclusive?" Robbie, the managing editor at Benevolence, a digital media company, asks while I type up my next blog. My dad's napping, so I must get as much done as possible. I imagine it's like having a toddler who needs to be entertained and supervised during all waking hours.

I stare at my phone screen for a second as if she can see me through the speaker. "I don't know how I feel because you're being too vague." My attention returns to the computer monitor.

She laughs. "Fair. A woman in Nashville saved a three-year-old, a six-year-old, and their family dog from drowning. She was injured in the process. A bystander on a bridge caught the rescue on his phone. It's going viral as we speak. I'll have my assistant book your flight and send you the rest of the details."

I chuckle. "I haven't given you my thoughts on doing the exclusive."

"It was a rhetorical question."

"Didn't sound like one." My fingers tap the keyboard.

"I know a nurse at the hospital. She said she can get you in to visit her, but they're not letting any press see her until she's discharged, which could be in the next few days."

"If I'm not the press and I'm not family, how is she getting me access to her?"

Robbie *tsks*. "Just pack a bag."

"As tempting as it sounds, I can't leave my dad."

"I thought you said he's better."

"I said he's no longer asking me to find his gun."

"So he's still suicidal?"

"No. He's messy."

She laughs. "I'm not following. You can't leave your dad for a day or two because he's messy?"

"Correct." I lean back in my chair and run my hands through my hair. "He doesn't flush the toilet or bathe without being told. He forgets to eat but never forgets to down a six-pack a day. And he recently discovered porn on the internet, but it only makes him cry."

Robbie snorts. "I'm sorry."

I can hear her failed attempts to suppress her laughter. "Jesus ... no wonder your mom left him."

"He wasn't like this when they were together. This is the result of her leaving. You know that part of a love story where one person says to the other, 'I'd be nothing without you'? This is my dad's version of being nothing without my mom. Is it a little extreme in my point of view? Absolutely. Am I judging him? Only slightly."

"I, uh ... I don't know how to respond, Eric. I need someone to cover this story. Are you still working with us? Or do I need to take your name off the list? I'm not trying to sound insensitive, but your dad's lack of personal hygiene and interesting use of pornography is not my issue. It doesn't sound like you're risking his life by leaving for a few days."

She's right. Still, I don't relish returning to several days of simmering despair and accumulated filth.

With a deep sigh, I mumble, "I'll go."

After the call, I fetch my bag and search for the viral video. When it starts to play, I toss my phone onto the bed and pack a couple of days' worth of clothes. The video isn't high-quality, but it's clear enough to see the woman straddling the fallen dead tree to pull the kids out of the water. The tree breaks when she tries to retrieve the dog, and she goes under.

"Dad?" I pause his porn and hand him a tissue, for his tears, of course. "I'll be gone for a couple of days. Call me if there's an emergency. I'm going to have the neighbors check in on you. I'll have your dinner delivered around six each night. Answer the fucking door when the food arrives. I'm rationing your beer, so if you drink it all in one day, you'll go without because I'm also taking away your car keys. Any questions?"

"Do you ... do you think," he stares at the paused screen, "that she'd take me back if I were open to that?" He nods at the computer. There are two men and one woman. It's bad enough that my parents' divorce has derailed my own life (not that I had big plans), but imagining my dad working in conjunction with another man (an old man) to do *that* to my mom, guarantees that I'll need therapy for the rest of my life.

"Mom is no longer with Francis. I've told you that a million times. I think she's decided to join a convent. Maybe you should start watching faith-based streaming networks, pray more, and wait for God to give you a new direction. In the meantime, shower, sober up, and don't forget to eat. Love you." I squeeze his shoulder and grab an Uber.

On the way to the airport, I get a text from Robbie's assistant with my flight and hotel information. Then she sends another text with the hospital and the name of the woman who saved the kids and the dog: Anna Black. I stare at it for several seconds before rewatching the viral video. The woman has on a ball cap, so there's nothing identifiable about her. Anna's not an uncommon name, and neither is Black. Still, I can't imagine it's her.

However, it only takes a few more minutes of going down the viral rabbit hole of that video before I see posts of her picture, the staff picture from when she worked at the bouldering gym in Des Moines.

"Shit," I say.

"Did you say something?" The Uber driver asks.

I shake my head. "Nothing."

● ● ● ● ●

HOURS LATER, I'm at the hospital looking for Robbie's nurse friend.

"I'm Kayla." She tucks her phone into the pocket of her scrubs. "I told Robbie I couldn't make any promises."

I smile through gritted teeth. Robbie omitted that tidbit of information.

"But her boyfriend just left to grab dinner, and her

parents are out of the country, so it's your lucky day. You can head to room 427, and I'll give you fifteen minutes before I kick you out and apologize to her for letting you slip past me. She's having surgery in the morning on her ankle, so please don't upset her."

I can't promise anything.

When I enter the room, Anna's leaden eyes open, and she blinks several times as if I'm not in focus. I wasn't sure how I would feel seeing her, but I didn't expect to feel it in my chest. She's not an interview or a story; she's the woman who ran her hands through my hair and kissed me before leaving me forever.

Holding up a vase of flowers, I smile since words fail me.

"Eric?" she whispers.

I set the vase on the windowsill. "Fancy seeing you here. What have you been up to? Just ... saving lives?" I turn back to her. Fuck ... I'm so nervous.

"W-what are you doing here?"

I clear my throat and prepare my spiel. It's a good one. Honest and to the point. "*The managing editor for Benevolence asked me to get an exclusive interview with the woman who saved two children and their dog from the river after she saw the video going viral. Imagine my surprise when, on my way to the airport, the ME's assistant sent me the hospital name along with yours.*"

But I can't say it. My words and every memory of her are stuck in my head.

"Eric?"

God, she's lovely. She's quite the sight, even in a hospital gown with messy hair and pale lips. "I, uh ..." I clear my throat. "I saw a viral video of your rescue." The second I finish my statement, I internally cringe. It's not a lie but only ten percent of the truth. I'm working on the other ninety. I'd get to the point if we didn't have a past.

"Viral video?"

Sliding my hands into my pockets, I step closer to her bed. "Of you rescuing the two kids and dog." My lips twist.

Anna gives me a sad smile, closing her eyes for a brief moment, long eyelashes resting on her pale cheeks. "Eric. Fucking. Steinmann."

It takes a few seconds to register her words. They're unexpected. I chuckle, tension fading from my shoulders while that thing in my chest puffs with pride. I'm perfectly content with my middle name being "Fucking" if Anna's the one doling out names. "Are you on pain medication?" She seems a little loopy.

"I think so." She sighs. "I never thought I'd see you again." She gives me a lazy once-over.

"I kinda gathered that after six months of ghosting me. Sorry, it took me a long time to get the message. Hope is rather addictive."

Whatever hint of a smile she had two seconds earlier disappears in a breath. "I was awful."

I shake off her comment. "It's in the past. I'm glad you're okay. *And* you're a hero."

She presses her lips together for a beat while deep lines crease her forehead.

"The nurse said your parents are out of the country."

"A cruise."

I nod.

"You came to see me after three years because of a viral video?"

"Yes."

"Why?"

"Can't a guy bring a girl flowers after she does something heroic?" I offer an innocent shrug and a convincing smile.

I'm an idiot. A word-fumbling, half-truth-telling idiot. The words were there, and I said them in my head with confidence and eloquence. Then I had a massive brain fart. I'm sure she didn't intend to snafu my well-thought-out speech with a single look, but that's what she did. So if this comes back to blow up in my face, it's her fault.

Anna blinks several times. It's slow and methodic, like my brain minus the methodic part. "After three years, you saw me on a video and came here just to give me flowers?"

"Affirmative." I give her a sharp nod as my half-truths veer off into a straight-up lie. My brain has gone rogue, and I don't see a reverse switch or a panic button.

Her face morphs into an indecipherable expression. Is she shocked? Shook? Surprised? Happy?

I have no clue.

"Were you..." her teeth scrape along her lower lip "...worried about me?"

This is where I come clean. Coming clean *should* have happened the second I walked into the room, but seeing her stirred up these weird feelings. I can't be a cold-hearted vulture searching for an exclusive story, not with our history. So here I am going down a rabbit hole because I don't want to seem uncaring—which I'm not. How do I tell her that I care about her, as any kind human would, yet I need her account of the story, which I will use to make my editor happy?

"Seeing you evoked a feeling of nostalgia, and it was an unexpected emotion considering how we ended."

She frowns while taking her turn in the hot seat. "I wanted to reply to your texts and return your calls, but I was too," she rubs her lips together and gazes out the window for a few seconds, "ashamed."

"Ashamed?"

"Yeah, Well, I was many things."

I start to respond, but I'm not sure what to say. "You need to rest. I can see that you're exhausted. We can talk later. Have they told you when you're going home?"

"The day after tomorrow."

"I'd love to catch up and hear all about your heroic act. Where do you live? Or do you live with someone?" Such as her boyfriend who left to get dinner?

"I have a roommate."

"A roommate. That's ... great. Would he *or she* mind if I stopped by to visit?"

After a long, distrusting pause, she shakes her head. "I suppose not, but ..."

"Great. What's uh..." I pull out my phone "...your address?"

Again, she hesitates before giving me her address.

"I'll text you. Is your number still the same?" As soon as I say it, I pinch the bridge of my nose. "Crap. I'm not sure I want to know that answer. I've enjoyed telling myself that you have a different phone number, and somewhere along the way, you lost mine."

She averts her gaze.

"But I'm guessing you have the same number." I blow out a long breath. "That's fine. That's cool. You win some; you lose some. Good luck with your surgery. We'll talk soon." I squeeze her hand.

She stares at my hand on hers. "It's ... weird seeing you," she murmurs.

I don't move my hand, even though I should. What if her boyfriend shows up? Has she told him about me? I highly doubt it. I'm the stray cat she ran over with her car and kept going without so much as a glance in her rearview mirror. I may be carrying a tiny grudge.

"Weird good or weird bad?" I ask.

"I don't know yet." She reclaims her hand and slips it under the blanket.

"Well, I think it's good." I end the conversation with a decided nod and exit before things get any more ... weird.

CHAPTER SIXTEEN

AFTER ONE BEER, I'm still not feeling confident about this assignment. After one beer, I feel like I should have told Robbie that interviewing Anna would be a conflict of interest.

However, after three beers, I think that Anna saving those two kids and their dog was fate—a cosmic event to bring us together.

And after four beers ... I think about the day she straddled my face while enacting the sex scene from her book, and that's when I decide it's time to make my way from the hotel bar to my room and sleep it off before I do something stupid like text her a photo of my dick. Nothing says, "I've thought about you every day for the past three years," quite like a phallus taken in portrait mode with the *Vivid Cool* filter.

I stare at the ceiling from my diagonal position on the bed and chuckle at my thoughts. Maybe my new motto should be: Don't Drink, Drive, or Dick Pic. It's as if I've forgotten the little nugget about her having a boyfriend. It's as if I've forgotten that my purpose for being here is business, not personal.

The following day, Robbie wants an update.

Robbie: Did u get the story?

Eric: In the process

Robbie: What does that mean?

Eric: I need some extra time

Robbie: But ur getting the exclusive, right?

Eric: Probably

Robbie: What does probably mean? What's the hold-up?

Eric: It's requiring a bit more finesse than I initially anticipated

Eric: She had surgery today. Hoping to get to talk to her tomorrow

Robbie: Don't blow this!

For the rest of the day, I evenly divide my time and mental energy between my past with Anna and the future—specifically, the physical state my father and house will be in when I return home.

The following morning my anticipation and anxiety hit a breaking point, so I text Anna.

> Eric: Hey! You home? Can I stop by for a visit?

> Anna: Anna's sleeping. Who is this?

"Great," I mumble, staring at my phone. That's right ... she has a boyfriend.

> Eric: A friend

> Eric: I told her I'd stop by today to chat. Please have her message me when she's awake

> Anna: ok

That was easier than I expected. Since she has the same phone, I have to assume I'm a name in her contacts. If she were my girlfriend, I wouldn't be "ok" with some guy friend texting her to get together.

Over the next two hours, I search for other videos of Anna's heroic rescue. Then she texts me that she's awake, and I toss my computer aside and head to her house. The neighborhood is middle to upper-class. Anna's doing well in her new job, or her boyfriend has nice housing perks.

I ring the doorbell of the two-story home and inspect the well-manicured yard while waiting for someone to answer.

"Hello. You must be Eric." A man greets me with a friendly smile. I'd guess he's at least in his mid-forties from the gray mixed into his dark hair.

"I am."

"Come in. I'm Shaun. Nice to meet you."

I step inside the entry and shake his proffered hand. "You too. Is this your place?"

"Yeah. I got it as a foreclosure. Last summer Anna helped me renovate the main level. She has impeccable taste."

I think about that comment for a second. "Mmm. How is she?"

"See for yourself." Shaun gestures for me to follow him.

Anna's in a leather recliner with a baseball game on the large television screen. She gives me a weak smile, much like the one she gave me at the hospital. I have a feeling she's still on pain meds.

"Surgery go well?"

"It did." She winces while trying to adjust in her chair.

"Anna, I will run to the store since your friend is here. Anything specific I can get you?" Shaun grabs his wallet and key fob from the kitchen island.

"That yogurt I like. You know which one?"

"Of course." He smiles at her. It's an endearing smile. It's the way Anna deserves to have someone smile at her.

For the record, I used to smile at her like that, but then I unknowingly took a shit on her book in front of her friends. So I suppose she never noticed my level of endearment.

"Raspberry or vanilla?" he asks.

"Both." She reaches for the glass of water next to her chair and takes a sip.

"Can you stay until I return?" Shaun asks me.

"Sure." I size him up the way he did to me when I arrived.

He gives me a high-chinned nod like he's watching me. Hell, he probably has indoor cameras in this place.

"Have a seat." Anna gestures toward the sofa while Shaun disappears out the back door.

"You live in a beautiful house."

She rubs her lips together and returns the water glass to the end table. "It's a great neighborhood."

"Shaun seems ... nice." I lift my ankle onto my opposite knee, going for casual yet confident—of which I am neither.

"He's the best. I don't know what I would do without him."

Must be nice. She clearly knew what to do without me—never look back.

While I comfort my bruised ego, Anna sighs. "I still can't believe you're here."

"About that. I, uh ... wasn't exactly forthright with you the other day."

"Oh?"

I rub the tension from my forehead. "I write for several online publications, and the managing editor at *Benevolence* asked me to get an exclusive interview with you. I didn't know it was you in the video until Robbie, the ME, had her assistant send me your name and the hospital. I nearly told her I couldn't do it, but then I ..."

Anna waits with an unreadable expression. "You?"

"I was curious. I wanted to know the story for myself, not the online publication. I wanted to know where you lived and why you moved away from Des Moines. And I wanted to know how you're doing. Did you write that great novel? Did you get married? Have kids? And ..." I shrug. "I knew if I told Robbie I couldn't do it, I would not be able to stop thinking about you. So here I am."

After a few seconds, Anna blinks and returns several slow nods.

"I ..." Shaking my head, I run my fingers through my hair. "I should have said all this at the hospital, but seeing you again messed with my thoughts. And you were groggy." I frown. "Much like today. So I didn't want to show up out of the blue and grill you about the incident, then leave just as quickly to write up a story as if seeing you didn't matter." I sound like an idiot. I'm talking so fast and grabbing whatever words pop into my head that Anna has to think I'm ... an idiot. It's the best word, maybe the only word.

"Do you want the story?"

Pausing my fidgety fingers and spinning thoughts, I relax because she's relaxed. Granted, she has the advantage of pharmaceuticals. "Yes. No. I don't even care now." I laugh. "Sorry. This isn't going how I thought it would go."

"How did you think it would go?" She cants her head.

"I thought I'd see you and things would feel … different. But they don't."

Her lips twist into contemplation for several seconds before her smile grows in tiny increments. "There's not much to tell, to be honest. I was out for a jog. I saw these kids straddling a dead tree hanging over the water. I didn't see any adults nearby. And by the time I jogged closer, one of the kids was in the water, holding on to a thin branch with one hand and the dog's collar with his other. The little girl was reaching for the boy. I yelled for her to hold on. And after that, I didn't give it much thought. I scooted along the fallen tree to help get the kids to safety. They were crying, upset about the dog struggling to get to the shore, so I made my way back along the fallen tree, just far enough to help the dog get out of the water. As I started to scoot backward, I heard a splintering sound, and in the next breath, I was under the water with my foot wedged between the tree and the rock. I swear I was on the verge of blacking out or dying. The panic. The pain. The burning in my lungs." She frowns and blinks back her tears. "And that's when I was rescued."

"Did you think to call 9-1-1 first?"

"I didn't have my phone, but I don't think I would have taken the time to call for help. It never even occurred to me. Shaun said a bystander called for help while I was trying to rescue the kids. Supposedly, the local news interviewed her."

I nod. "I saw the interview. I'm sure they'll also contact you soon for an interview."

Anna curls her hair behind her ear and then rubs her neck. "Then you'd better get your story online so you don't miss out on being the one with the exclusive interview."

"Doesn't matter," I say, leaning forward and resting my elbows on my legs. I mean it. It feels like an afterthought now that we're alone in the same room again. I remember how everything felt like an afterthought when we were together. I thought she was the one—the girl who would tame my wandering mind. In hindsight, I knew nothing.

"It has to matter," Anna says. "You got on a plane and flew here, the same day it happened, to get an *exclusive*. I bet your boss thinks it matters."

"She's not my boss. So ... tell me about Shaun."

Her eyes narrow. "Shaun?"

"Yeah." I sit back again, gaze wandering around the room. I can't sit still. I can't focus. I'm ... unsettled by these feelings.

"I've known Shaun for years. His girlfriend in high school used to babysit me. And he'd hang out too. It's such a small world. Shaun moved to Nashville a few years ago and started a real estate company."

"Do your parents like him?"

"Uh ... yeah. Why?"

"No reason. I mean ... I figured it might give them a moment's pause. You know?"

She rubs her lips together and hums. "I'm not sure

I do know. They moved to Florida shortly after I left Des Moines. They don't care where I live as long as I'm happy. If anything, they're thrilled that I'm figuring things out on my own."

"Hey. I'm not judging you." I hold up my hands. "Lord knows I've had the worst luck with relationships. So if you've found love and are happy, who cares what anyone else thinks about the age difference."

Anna's eyes widen, and a tiny gasp escapes her parted lips. "Wait. No. Shaun is not my boyfriend. Why would you think that?"

"Because the nurse at the hospital told me your boyfriend went to get dinner. And you live with a man and no other roommates, so I put two and two together."

"Um ... no." She wrinkles her nose. "That would be weird. After all, he essentially helped babysit me when I was seven."

"Well, he looks at you like he's your boyfriend. So if he's not, then why are you living with him?" I shake my head. "And ... you don't have to tell me anything. It's none of my fucking business."

Anna takes a drink of water and sets it back on the end table. "It's a crazy story. I took a job at an advertising firm here in Nashville—a dream job. And while looking for an apartment, I came across Shaun. He has rental properties, and I messaged him about one of his apartments. However, everything was out of my price range without a roommate. I didn't recognize his name, probably because I never knew his last name. But he asked if I was originally from Iowa because he recognized my name. Long story short, after several conversations, he offered to rent me a room here while I looked for a roommate. I was staying at a hotel because my job started immediately." She gives me a sheepish grin. "And I've just ... never moved out. I pay rent. I help around the house. Whenever I mention looking for my own place, he talks me out of it."

Since I'm not sure how to respond, I don't. I have so many questions, but they don't feel like mine to ask. "That's kind of him to be so ... kind." I have better words but never find the right ones with Anna. I'll never say the right thing.

A silence settles between us, and it magnifies the elephant in the room: did she stop writing? That question sits on the tip of my tongue, but I can't spit it out.

"Did you close your T-shirt shop?" She nudges the conversation in the right direction. Sort of.

"I still own it, but I don't manage it. I joined the family business, but it was bought out by a bigger ... business." Avoiding that elephant is tricky. Can I even say the word *publisher*? "My mom left my dad. And that's when I started blogging and freelance writing while keeping him from doing anything stupid. Well, more like irreversible."

"That's..." her face sours "...too bad. So you live with your dad?"

"Yes."

"Is that weird?" Anna chuckles.

With a sigh, I rub my face. "I wouldn't say the

living-with-my-dad part is weird. My dad's reaction to the divorce has been less than ideal."

"Ideal? What do you consider ideal?"

"That's probably not the right word. Maybe less than *typical*?"

"What do you consider a typical reaction to divorce?"

Here we go. I still can't say the right fucking word.

"So you're with an advertising firm. Do you like your job?"

Anna eyes me. If it takes her a few seconds to catch on to my change in subject, so be it. I'm not going down the same road with her.

Realization blooms in her cheeks. It's different. It's nice, I think.

"I'm sorry. It's the medication. I don't mean to interrogate you. It sounds like your dad's having a rough time. I'm sorry to hear that."

Where was this Anna three years ago? Oh, that's right. She was following her passion, and I was crushing her dreams like popping bubble wrap.

"When my parents had to live together without the distraction of work, my mom realized she had nothing to say to him. More than that, she decided she wanted to feel passion again. She's sixty-two. Is that too old to feel passion?" I lift a shoulder. "Who am I to say? All I know is that my dad didn't fight for her. He said he was 'too damn old and tired to chase ass.'"

Anna cringes.

"Yup. I can't imagine where I get my gift with words."

She bites her lips together.

"Clearly, he wasn't too old and tired to act like an ass."

Anna giggles. Her laughter still hits me in the feels. It's still my favorite sound.

"So she filed for divorce. And they stayed living together until the divorce was final. He seemed normal. Amicable with her. Nearly unaffected around me. He golfed with friends. Occasionally fished. Everything seemed good. Then the moving crew arrived to pack and load things into the truck. And, uh ..." I still can't say it without laughing. I love my dad, but I have no idea how he missed this. "He thought she was the one moving out. When he ignored the crew, holing up in his office, Mom had to instruct them as to which things were his and needed to be packed. He snapped when she opened his office door to tell him they were ready to take his desk and pack his books. Then he got arrested. Then he moved in with me after I bailed him out of jail, and Mom got a restraining order against him. Good times."

Anna covers her mouth.

"I know. There is no good response to that story."

She clears her throat. "How is he now?"

"It's all relative, so I'd say he's better. But I'll know more when I get home. This is the first time I've left him with nothing more than the neighbors checking in on him. He has little enthusiasm for life but no longer has a penchant for death, so I'm calling it progress."

"I ... I don't know what to say."

"Nothing. There is nothing to say. But really, tell me about your job."

And why did you stop writing? Was it my fault? Did I crush your dreams?

"I love my job. And I'm good at it. My boss is super chill. I have a great team. There's a lot of room for advancement. It's possibly the perfect job for someone with my skills. It's the dream job I imagined when I graduated from college."

I can't stop reading into every word, every tiny shift in her facial expressions. She's good at her job. Is she implying she wasn't good at writing? I can't imagine why she'd think that.

Because I'm an asshole.

"What about you? Do you like your job?"

I chuckle. "Yeah. It's fine. Admittedly, I'm still trying to figure out what I want to be when I grow up."

She smiles. It's kind and genuine. "How's that going?"

"Not so good. I keep coming to the same conclusion."

"What's that?"

I rub the back of my neck. "I don't want to grow up."

A burst of laughter fills the room, making me feel warm and comforted.

"I can't help it," I say, feeling embarrassed. "I'm not

motivated by work. I don't mind it. I do it because it's necessary. And my friends work, so it's a great way to pass the time until ..."

She snorts. "Until your friends can play?"

I return a guilty shrug. "Nothing beats a good climbing trip to Utah or Colorado. Mountain biking. Snowboarding. Concerts. If I can find a sitter for my dad, I'm always up for an adventure."

"Adulting *is* overrated. So is finding a sitter, I imagine."

"True on both accounts. But some of my friends are real adults now with marriage certificates and tiny humans destroying their houses. So I'm not the only one who has to find a sitter before heading out of town. The difference is that I can't hire the college girl down the street to stay with my dad."

"No?"

I shake my head. "My dad has *hobbies* that might offend other people, especially young women."

"What hobbies?" She gives me a curious expression.

"I can't go there. Some things about my dad are too embarrassing to share." Okay, I've told a handful of people, including Robbie, but I can't tell Anna. I care too much about what she thinks of me. And as much as it pains me some days, my father is an extension of me, or I am of him.

Anna stares out the window with slow blinks, leaving us with another awkward pause. It's suffocating. I want to ask about her writing. It's been three years. We've moved on with life. But I can't ask. And the fact that she doesn't mention it makes me feel like it's not a subject she's ready to discuss.

"Can I get you anything? Food? More water? If you're tired, go to sleep. I don't want to leave until Shaun gets back here."

Anna yawns. "I am exhausted. If I drift off to sleep, don't leave without waking me."

"Just rest." I retrieve my phone from my pocket and scroll through my messages. When I glance up, Anna's eyes are closed. I continue glancing through my messages, but my gaze keeps returning to her.

When Shaun returns, I lift my finger to my mouth. He nods while quietly lifting the bags of groceries onto the counter. Anna's zonked out. Not a twitch. When Shaun returns to the garage, I bend down and press my lips to Anna's cheek. "Bye, Anna Banana," I whisper.

When I approach the front door, Shaun pops his head around the corner. "Leaving?" he asks in a hushed tone.

"Yeah. She needs to rest."

"I hope you enjoyed catching up."

"I did."

"Anna told me you two dated before she left Des Moines." Shaun leans his shoulder against the wall.

I nod.

"She called you her biggest regret."

My brows lift. How am I to interpret that? Does she regret us? Or she regrets leaving? "I hope the good kind of regret if there's such a thing."

Shaun shakes his head. "I'm not sure. But she's focused now. In a better place." Shaun's face falls to a more somber expression. "She's a good person. Incredibly special."

I offer him a tight smile because I'm not sure how to respond to him. The way he delivers his words is cryptic. "Well, regret is a waste of time."

"It is." Shaun returns a stiff smile.

I open the door. "Take care of her."

"Always."

Always?

I take my exclusive story and stirred-up memories of Anna and head home to Kansas City and my roommate.

CHAPTER SEVENTEEN

Anna

"Where's Eric?" I rub my eyes.

Shaun glances over his shoulder from the kitchen island, where he's working on his computer and eating a sandwich. "He left."

"What?" I wince, trying to sit up straighter. "I told him to wake me before he left," I say to myself more than Shaun. My heart drops into my stomach.

"I'm sure he didn't want to wake you since you need to rest."

There was more to say. I didn't get to apologize for ... everything. I just needed to sleep off the drowsy effects of my pain meds.

Anna: U didn't wake me!

Anna: I told u to wake me before u left

Eric: U needed to sleep

Anna: I didn't get to say goodbye

Eric: I kissed u goodbye. We're good

I rub my lips together. He kissed me?

He kissed me ...

I stare at his message. *Are* we good? I can't imagine he means it. I was the world's worst girlfriend. Over the past three years, I've looked for a better label, but it always comes back to World's Worst Girlfriend. I have never been so ashamed in my life.

I type, delete, and retype my response.

Anna: ~~Was it a good kiss?~~

Anna: ~~I was the world's worst girlfriend. Sorry~~

Anna: ~~I regret so much that it deserves its own book~~

Anna: ~~Will I see u again?~~

Anna: ~~I forgot to ask. Do u have a girlfriend?~~

Anna: ~~Do u H8 me?~~

My phone rings. It's Eric.

"Hey."

"Say it," he says.

"Say what?"

"I'm tired of staring at three dots in a bubble. Then nothing. Then three dots. Again, nothing. You have a lot to say, but you're not saying it, at least not in a text. So say it. Tell me everything you've deleted in the past sixty seconds."

If he's been watching that texting bubble, that

means he's been thinking of me ... thinking of texting me or seeing if I've texted him since he left. That ignites a fire deep in my belly. Glancing over at Shaun working on his computer, I blow out a slow breath. "I'm sorry."

"For what?"

"For ... you know."

Eric chuckles. "You spent that long typing and deleting, and now I'm supposed to just *know?*"

"I'm mentally sluggish from the pain medication."

"It's..." he exhales, "fine."

"Your 'fine' sounds anything but fine."

"Anna, I spent six months saying everything I could think to say to you. I put *everything* out there, but you had no response. And I feel like you still don't have a response. And it's just frustrating."

"I knew you were mad."

"I'm not mad. I said I'm frustrated. Maybe I'm frustrated at myself."

"You sound mad."

Now I'm mad that he's mad. How did we have a cordial meeting at the hospital after three years and a friendly exchange when he was here a little over an hour earlier?

Shaun gives me a quick glance, concern lining his brow.

"It's not a good time," I say to Eric.

Silence.

"Eric."

"Time. Yeah, it's never a good time. Listen, I'll send

you a link to the story before it posts so you can approve any quotes."

"Eric?"

"What?"

I pinch the bridge of my nose and lose my nerve. Maybe I lose it because I *am* mentally sluggish. Maybe I lose it because Shaun can hear me. Or maybe I lose it because I'm not brave enough to say it. "Nothing," I whisper.

"Bye, Anna." He disconnects the call.

Leaning my head back, I close my eyes. What am I doing? I have nothing to lose. This is all on me. I need to own the past and the present.

Staring at my phone for a good ten minutes, I take the first step to right some wrongs.

> Anna: My deleted responses:

> Anna: Was it a good kiss?

> Anna: I was the world's worst girlfriend. Sorry

> Anna: I regret so much that it deserves its own book

> Anna: Will I see u again?

> Anna: Do u have a girlfriend?

> Anna: Do u H8 me?

I wait. And ... wait.

Nothing.

If this is payback for leaving him and ghosting him

for six months until he stopped trying to contact me, then that's fair. I deserve it and more.

"Everything okay, Anna?" Shaun asks. "Can I get you something? Yogurt? A sandwich? Do you need help getting to the bathroom?"

"Yeah," I murmur.

"To which one? Or everything?"

I don't register anything he's saying because Eric's giving me exactly what I deserve—what I've deserved for years. I should have been prepared for this but I never thought I'd see him again.

"Yeah," I whisper.

⁕ ⁕ ⁕

THE FOLLOWING DAY, I get a message from Eric with a link to the text of the exclusive interview. It's better than I expected. He makes me sound like a hero. I don't feel like one. I did what any decent human would do.

> Anna: I approve

> Anna: Thx for saying so many nice things about me. I don't feel deserving

Anna has an addictive personality. A kind soul ... The shiniest part of humanity ... Unforgettable ...

> Eric: I'll post it at five tonight

That's it. A robotic reply void of anything personal. Is the article just for show? For ratings? Does he believe the things he said about me?

I fish for another reply—for anything.

Anna: It was wonderful seeing u

Nothing.

I tell my heart it has no reason to feel blue, but it doesn't listen. It's mad too. I paid no attention to it the day I left Eric and hightailed it out of Des Moines. My heart didn't make that decision, neither did my brain. It was all ego. Egos are the demise of humanity. They're immune to true emotions and all reason. Egos don't know how to love. The ego eclipses everything good in life when we let it.

And I let it.

"Hey, honey!" My parents poke their heads into my bedroom.

I blink and clear my throat. "Hey."

"I'm so sorry we weren't here when you needed us. I hated knowing you were in surgery or could have ..." Mom chokes on her words.

"She's fine, dear." Dad rolls his eyes at my mom before hugging me. "But I'm so glad you're okay," he whispers.

"I'll plan my next bone-breaking accident for when you're in the country. How was your trip?"

"No. We're not talking about our trip yet. You tell me everything. What happened? How long will you be in a cast? Did the surgery go okay? Can you still do your job?"

My head explodes from her rapid-fire questions.

Dad waits with Shaun in the living room while Mom helps me wash up and dress. Then I tell them everything, except I leave out the Eric part.

CHAPTER EIGHTEEN

GASP!

I wake in the middle of the night, panicked and fighting for a breath. I'm crawling out of my skin. I need my cast off. It's … suffocating me.

I need to move my ankle, and I can't.

I can't move it, and I can't stop thinking I need to move it. Never have I felt so out of control—so out of my skin.

"Mom!" My heart races; my body trembles.

"What's wrong, honey?" Mom rushes into my bedroom from the guest bedroom across the hallway. Shaun steps into the room two steps behind her, pulling a T-shirt over his head.

"Anna?" He sounds as panicked as my mom.

"My foot. My foot! I need to move my foot." This is the most unnerving feeling. I'd give anything for someone to put me out of my misery. I reach for my foot, nearly falling out of bed.

"Does it hurt?" Mom asks while Shaun inspects my cast.

"No, it just ... I ... I need to move it."

"Shh ..." Wrapping her arm around me, my mom kisses the side of my head. "You're having a panic attack. Try to breathe through your nose slowly. Count with me. One. Two. Three. Four. Hold it ... Now, exhale. One. Two. Three. Four."

Shaun turns on the television. "Let's get your mind on something else. Okay?" He picks out a movie we've watched together and plays it.

I breathe in ... and out. And my mom keeps breathing with me, rubbing my back, stroking my hair. And eventually, I fall back to sleep.

Over the following weeks, I have nightly panic attacks, and my mom does her thing to help me through them. Shaun suggests I see my doctor to get something, but I don't want to take any more medication.

I feel myself slipping into a depression because I'm so tired of feeling this way and hobbling around on crutches. And as if the universe knows I need something, I get a text.

Eric: The kiss was good. Nothing creepy

Eric: U weren't the world's worst girlfriend. U weren't even MY worst girlfriend

Eric: If u write that book of regrets, I'll
read it. And I'll give it five stars

Eric: Ur seeing me again right now

He sends a picture of himself. It's a goofy, toothy mugshot.

I laugh. It's been too long since I've laughed.

Eric: I don't think I have a girlfriend.
No one I've asked to go steady

Eric: I could never h8 u

How do I respond? I'm as giddy as can be, nearly shaking with excitement.

Anna: Thank you <3

Eric: UR welcome

"What's that look all about?" Mom asks, glancing up from her book.

"What look?" Even while I speak, I can't wipe the grin from my face.

"Must be that Eric guy," Shaun says from his usual perch at the kitchen island. He sounds a little grumpy about it.

When I shoot him the evil eye, he winks. Okay, he's not grumpy.

"Who's Eric?" Mom asks.

Here's the thing ...

I told no one about B. Ashton except Eric. No

reason. She died. We ended. There was no need to further my embarrassment.

"Do you remember when we lived in Des Moines, and I dated a guy who liked climbing, but he didn't like my favorite book?"

"Wait. What?" Shaun completely turns around.

I ignore him. This isn't any of his beeswax.

Mom twists her lips. "Yeah, sort of."

"Well, he's a blogger slash journalist now, and he got the assignment to get an exclusive interview with me about saving those kids. We didn't exactly end on good terms, so things were awkward, but I think we're good now."

"He's the reason you were smiling like that?" Mom gives me a knowing grin.

"I wasn't smiling *like* anything. I was just smiling. A pleasant expression. No big deal."

"Let's back up. Is that why you and Eric broke up? He didn't like your favorite book?" Shaun prods.

"Don't you have work to do?" I give him a tight grin.

"Nope. I'm all caught up and all ears."

Mom rolls her eyes. "Anna broke up with him because she got a job offer in Nashville. Right, honey?" She has so much trust in her eyes.

Shaun ... not so much.

"It's not uncommon for differing points of view to be dealbreakers in relationships," I say like it's no big deal.

"I'm not following," Mom says, sliding a bookmark into her book and setting it aside.

"She broke up with a guy over a book." Shaun chuckles. My roommate has come to know me too well.

"Not *a* book." I cover my face with my hands. "My book," I mumble.

"What are you talking about?" Mom asks.

My hands flop to the arms of the recliner. "Do you remember I had you read my favorite book, *The Last Person* by B. Ashton?"

She nods. "Yeah, I vaguely remember. I can't remember if I liked it."

"You didn't." I frown. "I am ... *was* B. Ashton."

They say nothing. I get empty stares and heavy blinks. I would react similarly if my mom told me she wrote a novel I didn't know about.

"You published a book?" Shaun breaks the silence.

"I self-published a book. Then in a weak moment, my insanity bred with my ego, and I made the most regrettable decision to submit it to a publisher." I frown. "Actually, that wasn't the most regrettable decision I made. *That* would have been the day I decided to choose my book for the book club at our apartment, but I didn't tell anyone."

My poor mother looks betrayed, and it feeds this recently resurrected guilt.

"Let me get this straight. Eric didn't like a book he didn't know you wrote?" Shaun asks.

I nod.

"Anna ... you ... you wrote a book?" Mom stutters

past her confusion. "Why didn't you tell me and your dad?"

"At first, I was afraid that no one would like it, hence using a pen name and self-publishing it. I was testing the waters. Then I got some good reviews on the book, so I decided to submit it to a publisher. By then, I wanted to wait for a reply from the publisher before I told anyone. It *killed* me to keep it a secret. I spent an insufferable amount of time writing the story. It felt like a part of my soul resided in those pages."

"Honey, I'm sorry if I didn't say good things about it. I feel like a terrible mother, like I should have somehow known it was your book."

I shake my head. "It was fiction. How would you have known?"

"How did Eric find out?" Shaun sits on the opposite end of the sofa as my mom.

I grunt, feeling something between laughter and tears building inside of me. "I like to call it the worst luck imaginable, but I'm sure it could be a classic case of divine intervention. Eric's parents owned the publishing company where I submitted my manuscript. I had to find a publisher who would accept a submission directly from an author without going through a literary agent. Eric occasionally helped his parents go through the slush pile. Guess whose manuscript was in that pile?"

They share a wide-eyed gaze.

"We never discussed his parents' business. He never told me about his side gig. It was lack of communication and..." I sigh, "...a terrible lie on my part. A lie of omission. And that lie ruined us."

"Because you couldn't handle him not liking your book?" Shaun asks.

"Yes. No." I shake my head. "I was too invested in my book. As I said, I felt like it held a piece of my soul. And I knew I would always feel like he didn't love that part of my soul. When I left him, I felt like a failure in every way imaginable."

"Oh, Anna ..." Mom scoots to the sofa's edge and rests her hand on my good foot. "You are not a failure. You wrote a book. That's huge, honey."

"It felt huge. Not so much anymore. I walked away from a great guy because I couldn't separate myself from my work."

"Maybe this is a second chance." Leave it to my mom to look for a silver lining.

"It's complicated. I'd love to meet him for the first time now. But he'll always know what happened, and so will I. And he lives in Kansas City. It wasn't meant to be. I think it is a chance to reconcile the past. Nothing more."

CHAPTER NINETEEN

Eric

Eric: Walking?

Anna: Hi! Not yet

Anna: Today I got a boot. My mom
left two weeks ago

Anna: I'm a pro with crutches

IT'S BEEN weeks since I messaged her. I thought she'd keep the conversation going, but she didn't. So here I am ... itching to talk to her.

Eric: I need a video of this new "pro"fession

Minutes later, my phone chimes. It's a video of Anna in shorts, a tee, her boot, and a massive smile while navigating a flight of stairs.

Eric: Now ur just showing off

Anna: Lol. I'm sweating. Stairs are a beast. I'm sure u saw me pitting out

I grin.

Eric: U look pretty today

I watch the typing bubbling appear and disappear over and over.

Eric: Say it

Anna: Don't say those words. I'm too vulnerable

Eric: Why?

Anna: Immobility = depression. I've had so much anxiety—panic attacks

Anna: When my mom was here, she helped me through them

Anna: Since she's been gone, I've had to deal with them alone

Eric: Sorry to hear that. U still look pretty

Anna: (crying emojis)

Eric: (hug emojis)

Anna: Sorry

Anna: Shaun's mom is in the hospital.
So he's in Maine for who knows
how long

Anna: It's quiet. I'm going crazy

Anna: Of course it's my right leg so I
can't drive

Anna: Yesterday I paid an Uber driver
to take me for a ride

Anna: Just a ride (laughing
emoji/face-palm emoji)

Eric: Wanna FaceTime?

Anna: Sure

She answers her call on the first ring. "Hi."

"Hi." I can't hide my grin. Her hair's in braided pigtails.

"When do you start physical therapy?"

Anna sighs, blowing her bangs out of her face. "Next week."

"Tell me about the anxiety."

She proceeds to tell me about her panic attacks. We talk for over an hour, and I have to end it because I have a podcast interview.

"This was fun. You have no idea how much I needed to have a face-to-face conversation with someone besides my mom. Freya's pregnant and refuses to FaceTime with me because her face is too puffy."

"Well, I'm your guy. Anytime you want to see my

handsome face, it's yours."

"I see you haven't lost an ounce of confidence."

"Yeah, right. That's why it took me so long to tell you why I visited you after your accident."

"True." Her lips twist.

"Take care." I give her a cheesy wave.

She mirrors my cheesy wave, but it doesn't look cheesy coming from her.

Once an idiot, always an idiot.

A real job with a real boss would be useful when I get hair-brained ideas like this one.

"I think you need out of the house," I casually tell my dad while unloading the dishwasher.

"You're kicking me out?" he asks from my recliner that he's claimed as his own.

"Not yet. I'm suggesting a trip. When's the last time you took a trip?"

"When She kicked me out."

She, with a capital "S," is my mom. Although, he's consistent and says "Her" with a capital "H" when necessary. I miss my parents, Bill and Alice. Now I'm dealing with She/Her and Man Child. Yes, my mom refers to my dad as Man Child because he lost all rights to be a grown man after throwing a tantrum the day she moved him out.

"Since your last big trip was to jail, I think you're due. How do you feel about Nashville?"

"You're sending me to Nashville? Do I look like someone who knows how to line dance?"

I shake my head with a silent chuckle. "I can't answer that until we get you some boots and a proper hat."

"I've got bad knees. You know that. One wrong move, and I could be ass over ears. What about Vegas? We could rent one of those stripper buses like Warren did for his son's fortieth birthday."

"There were twelve of us on that trip. I'm just talking about the two of us."

"We've got the means. Who cares if it's just the two of us."

I steal the remote from the arm of his chair and shut off the TV. "There's a woman I want to visit in Nashville. I'll put you up in a nice hotel since *we have the means*. But you have to promise to be on your best behavior. Shower. Eat. Act like the grown man you are."

"You're flying to Nashville to get laid? Surely you can get laid locally. It's better for the environment."

Resting a fist on my hip, I stare at the ceiling. "She's a friend. And she's alone and on crutches from an accident. I can tell she's having a rough time since her roommate's out of town. I want to help her out for a few days."

"Then I'll stay here."

"The last time I was gone, Talia Johanssen called the police because you got the mail ... naked."

"You know that's not what happened. It was an Amazon package—"

"In the mailbox?"

He frowns, squinting his eyes. "And I wasn't naked. I was wearing boxers."

"You were drunk and wearing them on your head."

He lifts a shoulder and drops it. "I was wearing underwear. That's the truth."

"I'll pack your bag. Now, go take a shower. We can get an eleven-twenty flight tomorrow."

CHAPTER TWENTY

WHEN THE PLANE lands in Nashville, I check my dad into a hotel and order him room service.

"I'm probably staying the night with Anna, so don't wait up. And by don't wait up, I mean lights off, TV off, and the laptop shut by eleven. I'll be back in the morning to check on you."

"You're going to get some whoopie with a girl on crutches?" He whistles. "Good for you, son. Just be careful. The last thing we need is you getting sued and losing more of this family's money."

I'm speechless.

I shouldn't be by this point, but I am. My dad used to be a stand-up guy. A shrewd businessman. A well-respected publisher. A loving husband. A devoted father.

Now he's … I don't even know.

"Call me if you need anything that's a true human necessity."

He plops onto the bed and turns on the TV. "Well, that's open to wide interpretation."

"It's not," I say before shutting the door behind me.

ANNA OPENS her door after several knocks. Her glossed lips part while she balances on one leg and crutches. After a few seconds, her gaze slides to the backpack in one hand and then to the petal-less bouquet of stems in my other hand.

"What ..." The trail of petals on the sidewalk behind me steals her attention. "What are you doing here?"

"I have no idea. One minute I was texting you. The next I was FaceTiming. And in the next breath ... I was boarding a plane to Nashville." I shrug. "Are you busy? I can come back another time."

Shock still dominates her face, but she grins after a few more seconds. "I have a little free time to spare." She hobbles backward a few feet to let me inside.

I set my bag on the floor and the stems on the banister. "Are you up for a drive? Or have you and an Uber driver already gone on a date?"

Anna laughs, and I instantly think of anything to keep her laughing. I've missed it so much.

"If you're calling my outing with an Uber driver a date, then it implies that you taking me for a drive would be a date." She leans forward a fraction, putting more weight on her crutches. "Did you fly to Nashville to take me on a date?"

"Do you need help getting to the car?"

We have a stare-off.

"I do not."

I glance over her shoulder at the artwork on the wall. How did I miss it the first time? Her gaze follows mine to the oil-painted portrait of an old woman.

"You like it?" she asks.

"It's ... well, no offense to your friend, but it looks a little juvenile."

"Juvenile?"

I nod. "Like a child painted a portrait of their grandmother in seventh-grade art class. But hey, art is very personal. I'm sure Shaun fell in love with it."

"Juvenile?" she says slowly.

I shrug and nod; then it hits me. "Oh, don't tell me, he has a child who painted it?"

Anna stares at the painting. "No. I picked it out during the remodel. I fell in love with it at an art expo downtown."

Fuck my life.

"Well, it was nice knowing you." I pick up my bag and reach for the door handle.

"Where are you going?"

I pause, hanging my head. "I never say the right thing. I'm always saying the wrong word to you. And it's always an unintentional insult. I should stop speaking. There's a reason I'm single. I don't know how to keep my mouth shut."

"I'm not offended," she says.

When I get the nerve to face her, she smiles.

"You don't have to like my taste in art. In music. Food. *Books* ..."

"But I don't have to show my distaste for things you like outwardly."

"True." Anna smirks. "But you said it yourself; it's unintentional. So let's go. I need out of here." She nods toward the door.

After pausing to let my reluctance work its way out of my conscience, I open the door for her, and we take a drive. She rolls down the window and lets the wind tangle with her blond hair.

Eyes closed.

Lips bent into a beautiful smile.

After miles of nothing but the wind and radio filling the space around us, I take the next exit and pull into Wendy's.

"What are you doing?" Anna opens her eyes and lifts her head.

"I'm feeling a Frosty."

"A Frosty?"

"Yeah. Want one?"

"Uh ..."

"It's one of the five original menu items. A classic." I lower the window to order. "Two Frosties."

"And a small fry." Anna shrugs. "What are you going to dip in the Frosty?"

I chuckle, turning toward the speaker. "And a large fry."

"You know, there are a bunch of great places to get ice cream here."

"But only one place to get my favorite Frosty."

"Is it a little odd that you know the Frosty is one of Wendy's original five menu items?"

"Not at all." I wait for the car in front of us to pull away from the window.

We get our Frosties and fries and park in the lot. Anna dips a fry into her Frosty, and I do the same.

"I'm supposed to be working," she says. "I asked for more work because I've been going stir-crazy."

"And I've derailed your day?" I offer her an apologetic frown around my straw. "I'll take you home after we're done here, and I'll leave you to get your work done."

"Leave me? And go where?"

"Home."

"Stop." She giggles. "You can't fly to Nashville just for a drive and a stop at Wendy's."

"I can. It would serve me right for showing up unannounced."

"You showing up unannounced is the best thing that's happened to me since the last time you showed up unannounced."

I bite back my automatic brush-off of her compliment. Instead, I use my next breath to say everything I've already said in a text. Maybe it will land better now that we're face-to-face. Or maybe it will mean more because so much time has passed. "Anna, I've had so much time to think about this. I've tried to say it a dozen ways, hoping one way might resonate and make things better. What happened between us was unavoidable. I know why you didn't tell me it was your book—"

"Eric—"

"No." I shake my head. "I have to say this. It wasn't anyone's fault. It was natural for me to have an opinion of something that seemed inconsequential. But it was just as natural for you to feel heartbroken because it was anything but inconsequential to you. I wish I had seen it clearer, but I was too invested in us. I was angry that something was coming between us. And all I could see was that it was 'just' a book. I felt betrayed, but I didn't know why. You weren't trying to lie to anyone. You were taking a risk that felt necessary to you. And I see that now. But I deeply regret taking out my frustration over us on your manuscript. I regret making you feel like anything less than a talented and brave person for following your dreams. Every word I said was wrong—most were unintentionally wrong. But there were words exchanged that I wish I could take back even though I know it wouldn't have changed our outcome. And for those words, I'm so sorry."

She stirs her Frosty with a fry; it's so soaked I think it might break off and drown. "I was ..." She lifts her gaze, a blank stare aimed at the car parked in front of us. "I was immature. My ego engulfed everything and everyone around me. And I was blinded by the feeling that I left a part of myself in that story. I couldn't see the forest through the trees. I couldn't separate myself from the book. So I knew—I thought I knew—that you really didn't like me if you didn't like this..." she shakes her head, closing her eyes "...this thing that felt like a part of me that *I* loved so much."

I nod several times.

"It felt like ..." Anna chuckles. "It felt like you thought I was nice, and we had a few things in common, and you liked my body, but you didn't really like my personality." Her nose scrunches when she glances at me. "But over the past three years, as I've thought about it—and I've thought about it a lot—I imagined discovering that you loved to sing. It was your passion. And you felt like it expressed your soul. But when you sang for me, I thought you sounded awful."

I don't know where she's going with this, but it's amusing.

"I wouldn't have liked you any less. But it would have been hard for me to support your quest to become a rock star wholeheartedly. Does that make sense?"

I shove a wad of fries in my mouth and mumble, "You don't think I'm a good singer?"

She snorts before sipping her Frosty. "I don't know. I haven't heard you sing."

"Such a crime. I'm pretty good. I can slay Josh Kerr's *Backseats and Burnt CDs*."

Anna's head tips back in laughter. "Oh my gosh ... I needed this. And I'm sure you're a great singer. You haven't decided what you want to be when you grow up because you can do anything." Her laughter simmers, but her grin remains.

It feels warm in my chest, a high like climbing the face of a mountain and standing at the top.

❚❚❘❘≡❘❘❘／❘❘❘≡❘❘❘❘

WHEN WE RETURN to the house, Anna steps out of the car and hops on one foot to retrieve her crutches from the back seat.

"I could have gotten those for you."

"My Uber driver doesn't." She shoots me a goofy grin over the roof of the car.

"Oh, Anna, I hope you don't give him a second date if he doesn't show more chivalry."

She unlocks the front door. "How did your chivalrousness slip my mind?"

"That's an excellent question."

As soon as Anna reaches the recliner, she collapses with a long sigh. I peruse the room's perimeter, inspecting everything on the walls and shelves, but I don't say anything. Words get me into trouble with Anna. And I didn't make the trip to offend her. I'm not sure why I made the trip, but I'm here, and there's no place I'd rather be.

"I'm going to finish a project that's due in the morning. It should take about an hour. If you brought your suit, you can swim."

Facing her, I slip my hands into my pockets. "No suit."

"You could borrow one of Shaun's."

"I'll pass. I'm not a fan of swim briefs."

With a snort, she narrows her eyes. "What makes you think he wears swim briefs?"

"Just a hunch."

She shakes her head, a blinding smile on her face. We stare at each other. Explanations have been given. Apologies have been exchanged. Yet, there's something we're still ignoring.

"I can't believe you're here."

I shrug it off like I was in the neighborhood and just decided to drop by. "What if I raid the fridge and make us something for dinner?"

"Sure. Good luck with that. I've been ordering takeout since Shaun left."

I have no idea what's in the kitchen, but I'm determined to make a great meal out of something.

Over the next hour, I busy myself in the kitchen while Anna works on her computer, headphones covering her ears. I hand her a bowl when she slips them off her head and closes her computer.

"Where did you get the pasta?" She stares at the plate.

"Not from the pantry." I fake a frown while sitting on the sofa with my bowl. "There was a jar of pasta sauce but no pasta. How does that happen?"

She eyes the pasta and then glances up at me again. "So ... where did you get the pasta?"

"I made it."

"What?"

I shrug, twirling the pasta around my fork. "I made it."

"You *made* it?"

"Of course. It's three ingredients."

Anna looks like I told her water isn't wet. "We don't have a pasta maker."

"I'm the pasta maker. I made the pasta. It's called two hands, a rolling pin, and a knife. Any more questions?"

Taking a bite, she chews it slowly. "It's ... good."

"It's okay. The jarred sauce isn't the most complementary but works in a pinch."

"You're full of surprises." She grins after licking sauce from her lips.

Two things get confirmed by her reply.

One: I like surprising her.

Two: I like it when she licks her lips.

CHAPTER TWENTY-ONE

Anna

Everything this man does is a mating dance.

His smile.

His chivalry.

His spontaneity.

His surprising love of Wendy's Frosties.

And ... he made pasta.

I would *never* think of making my pasta, so his idea of simplicity is my idea of going the extra *ten* miles.

"Is it too presumptuous of me to sleep on the sofa? I can get a hotel room." He yawns, glancing at his watch. It's nearly eleven.

"You can sleep anywhere you want." I lower the recliner and sit up straight. When I lift my gaze, Eric gives me a raised brow.

I bite my lips together. "That sounded a little too ..."

"Welcoming? Suggestive? Sexual? Tempting?"

"Stop." I laugh. "You and your one-word replies are too much."

"Do you need help getting to sleep?"

"Help?"

He scoots to the sofa's edge and rests his elbows on his knees. "Help to get up the stairs? Help to get into your pajamas? Help going to sleep?"

Standing, I rest my weight on my crutches. "I'm good. You can sleep in the bedroom across from mine. Pinstriped comforter. I can shut off the lights from my phone."

He eyes me as if I might have a different answer.

"Night, Eric."

"Night, Anna."

I hobble up several stairs and glance over my shoulder as he retrieves his bag by the front door. "Thank you."

"For what?"

"For being here. For saying everything you said. And for listening." I sigh. "Seriously, *for listening*. You have no idea how much I needed to apologize ... to explain my actions. A weight lifted. I didn't realize how heavy that weight of guilt was until today. I never thought I'd see you again, so I shoved everything to the back of my mind like one does when they lose someone before saying everything they wanted to say."

With a concentrated expression, he nods several times.

"Well, that's all," I murmur.

When I emerge from the bathroom, Eric's in the guest room with the door shut. I close my door and climb into bed, turning on the TV to distract my runaway thoughts until I fall asleep.

Several hours later, I shoot to sitting, choking on a gasp. I *hate* this anxiety. It's more debilitating than my injury. If it's not the need to move my ankle, it's the feeling of my lungs burning with the need to breathe when I was trapped under the water. Sweat trickles down my back and between my breasts. I tear off my shirt.

"Anna?"

I startle, hearing Eric's voice.

"Wh-what are you doing?" I pull my sheet over my naked chest.

He's on the floor with a pillow, blanket, jogging shorts, and no shirt.

"When did you come in here?"

"When I thought you were asleep." He sits on the edge of the bed, brushing my hair away from my face. "I wanted to be here if you woke up."

I glance at the T-shirt I discarded to the floor. "Why are you being so nice to me?" I whisper while tears burn my eyes. This isn't how I wanted him to see me.

"Anna?" He cups my cheek with his hand.

I shift my gaze from the T-shirt to him.

"All I've ever wanted is to be nice to you."

I blink, letting the emotions spill over my cheeks. "I'm s-still so a-ashamed for how I t-treated you."

"No," he whispers, keeping his hand pressed to my cheek while his lips press to my other cheek.

I freeze, and so does he.

My breaths leap over each other until I reach a solid pant.

Something's buzzing, a vibrating sound. Eric deflates a fraction, bowing his head. The vibrating noise continues. With a sigh, he squats by my bed and retrieves his phone.

"Hey, what's wrong?" he says, holding his phone to his ear. After a few seconds, he rubs his temple. "It's the middle of the night. Why aren't you asleep?"

Another long pause.

"You'll just have to make it work. What do you expect me to do at this hour?" Eric scratches the back of his head, then claws at his hair and grumbles. "Stick a pillow between your legs."

I hear a voice on the other end, but I can't make out what's being said.

"There's probably a complementary bottle you can use. Check the bathroom. Good night." Eric tosses his phone on the blanket by his pillow. He takes a few long breaths before sitting on the edge of my bed again.

"Everything okay?" I ask.

"My dad doesn't have his pajamas."

"Where are they?"

Eric pinches the bridge of his nose. "At home."

"Isn't *he* at home?"

"He's at a hotel."

"Why is he at a hotel?"

"Because I thought he needed to get out of the house."

"You kicked your dad out and sent him to a hotel?"

He laces his fingers behind his neck. "He's at a hotel here in Nashville."

My face scrunches. "Your dad's here? In Nashville? And you're ... with me?"

"Correct."

"Eric, that's ..."

"It's fine."

"It's not fine. He's calling you in the middle of the night; clearly, it's not fine."

"I forgot to pack his pajamas. He's a guy. He can sleep in his boxer shorts."

"Doesn't seem like he can."

Eric chuckles. "He likes to sleep in long pants because it prevents chafing on his inner thighs. Apparently, he moves around a lot in his sleep. Now he's worried his legs will be chafed in the morning, and I didn't pack lotion for him."

"Eric." I cover my mouth to muffle my laughter while my other hand keeps the sheet to my chest. "You need to go be with your dad. You don't have to stay with me. Really."

"He's fine." Eric sounds so exasperated, and it's kind of funny. It's kind of cute.

I can't believe he brought his dad with him just so he could see me again.

"What can I get you?" he asks, resting his hand on my leg.

"Um ..." I nod toward the floor. "You can get my shirt for me."

He glances over his shoulder at my shirt and then turns back to me. "I like your shirt on the floor."

I shake and shiver with a nervous laugh. "Eric," I murmur.

"Anna ..." He scrapes his teeth along his lower lip while tugging at the sheet, inching it down my chest a little more with each tug until my breasts are exposed, nipples hard and sensitive. With his eyes on me, he ducks his head until his lips are at my nipple. I feel his warm breath on my flesh, and I swallow hard. But he doesn't move. It's as if he's waiting for permission. Breathing is its own challenge; if he thinks I can eke out a single word, he's crazy.

Instead, I run my fingers through his hair, and that's all the permission he needs. I almost fall apart when his lips cover my nipple.

When his hand cups my breast.

When his other hand rests high on my leg where the sheet's fallen to the side.

What are we doing? Where is this going? Does it have anywhere to go? Do *we* have anywhere to go?

"E-Eric ..."

"Hmm?" He hums over my breast.

"I'm ... I'm in a boot."

His gaze lifts to mine. "Do you want me to stop?"

It's an unfair question for several reasons. I'm in nothing but a flimsy pair of panties. He's shirtless. I can't walk without crutches, yet we're discussing sex.

At least, I think that's implied. And when he asked me if I wanted to stop, the pad of his thumb teased the crotch of my panties.

I gulp with a tiny headshake.

Eric grins, and his tongue teases my nipple again. Then it flicks my navel. I ease back onto my elbows as he brings my good leg to the side to wedge his torso between my spread legs.

"I'm sorry you have anxiety," he says while his lips ghost along my stomach to my hip, where his fingers curl into the waist of my panties, pulling them down my legs.

"It's okay ..." I whisper despite his hands and lips stealing my voice.

When he can't move my panties past my boot, he frees them from my good leg and leaves them dangling below my other knee.

I haven't shaved anywhere in weeks, so I'm conflicted. Should I feel desired knowing that he wants me even with my ungroomed parts? Or should I feel embarrassed?

"Je ... sus ..." My hips jerk when his tongue slides between my spread legs.

Desired. I'm going with desired.

A hairless body is overrated. Why do women try so hard? I've never encountered a man who gives a shit.

Eric's slow and methodic. He's deliberate with each stroke, like with every thrust of his lower body into the mattress. My good foot rests on his ass, and every time his glutes squeeze, I come closer to orgasming. I collapse onto my back, twisting side to side, pumping my pelvis against his mouth.

Broken ankle. What broken ankle?

Anxiety. What anxiety?

He crawls up my body. When his lips tease my ear, he whispers, "Can I go further?"

"Y-yes." I claw his back. The tickle of his chest teasing my nipples makes my legs shake.

With an impatient hand, he shoves down the front of his shorts and briefs and plunges into me like a man who hasn't had sex in years. I don't dwell on how long it's been. I'm not stupid. I know I wasn't his last sexual encounter.

He groans while his tongue probes the inside of my mouth. My knees draw toward my chest. It's an indescribable feeling. My doctor should have prescribed sex instead of the pain meds that had me yoyoing between grogginess and uncomfortably irritated.

"You're goddamn perfection," he says through labored breaths over my mouth before kissing me again.

Perfection?

So many emotions surge through my body and settle in my chest from that one word. Three years ago, I thought he was *almost* perfect.

I haven't felt this level of euphoria in a long time. Endless weeks of pain, anxiety, and depression have plagued me. I yell, "Dear god, yes," and fall into a limp pile of flesh and bones.

Eric collapses, his body weight pinning me to the

mattress while he chuckles with his face buried in my neck. "Dear god, yes ..." He repeats my words as if nothing has ever given him such satisfaction.

I grin even though he can't see it. Should I be embarrassed that I'm so vocal? Maybe. I'm too busy being thankful that Shaun isn't here. I wouldn't be able to look him in the eye ever again.

"Thank you," I say, catching my breath. "I needed that."

Eric's body shakes with light laughter. "You don't ever have to thank me for ... that."

"Well," I feather my fingers along his back, "you deserve something—a medal, a gold star. Maybe a cookie bouquet. At the very least ... a high five."

More laughter vibrates his body before he eases off me. "How's your ankle?" Concern lines his face while he pulls up his briefs and shorts.

"Fine." I sit up. "Can you hand me my shirt now?"

He plucks my shirt off the floor and turns it right side out before sliding it over my head and helping me thread my arms through it.

"Thank you."

"Need help getting to the bathroom?"

"Nope." I stand and slide my crutches under my arms more confidently than one should be, with their panties hanging from their boot.

Eric stands in my way, giving me a funny look.

"Excuse me," I say.

He holds up his hand. I stare at it. What is he doing?

"High five."

I try hard to keep a straight face, but it's impossible. After all, I *did* suggest the bare minimum of a high five. "Well done." I slap his hand.

He grins. Then he steps aside so I can clean up and piece myself back together.

"So ..." I steal his attention away from his phone when I return. "That, uh ... happened."

Eric gives me a reassuring smile, instantly putting me at ease. "I regret nothing."

"I'm not on the pill."

He maintains his smile, but his Adam's apple bobs and his eyes widen slightly.

"Still no regrets?"

It takes him a few seconds, but he manages to ease his head side to side in tiny increments.

"I'm not leaving my job. You'll have to move here. Or we can have shared custody, but I plan on breast-feeding for at least a year, so you can't have our baby in Kansas City until she's weaned." I sit next to him and prop my crutches against the nightstand.

"Why would I live in Kansas City if my baby's here?"

"Your job. Family. Friends." I scoot around to get my legs under the sheet.

Eric eyes me when I lay my head on the pillow, demanding my full attention. His expression softens, and he shuts off the lamp by my bed and crawls next to me, enveloping me in his arms while kissing my head. "Why do you think it's a girl?"

"That's your response? Not an apology? Not an ounce of panic? Are you kidding me?"

"You *thanked* me. We high-fived. Now I'm supposed to apologize and panic?"

"I'm on the pill," I mumble in defeat. "But would it kill you to show a little more responsibility?"

"I know you're on the pill. They're on your nightstand."

How is he still one-upping me?

CHAPTER TWENTY-TWO

Eric

I WAKE at five and untangle Anna's body from mine. I'm pretty sure her boot permanently indented my shin. When I'm showered and dressed, I peek into her bedroom, but she's still asleep—not a flinch. I'm not sure how that happened last night; it just did. Everything with her seems to happen without much thought. When I'm with her, I want to touch her, kiss her, consume her. It's been that way since the day we met, and three years didn't do anything to change that. I'd like to stare at her until she opens her eyes, but I have to check on my dad.

He's an early riser but not an actual morning person. And I fear he could be in a bad way this morning after a night without his pajamas. However, he's nowhere to be found when I open the hotel room door.

"Dad?" I call his name as if he's hiding behind the curtains or in the shower with the light off. He's not. "Where the hell are you?" I mumble, glancing at the locator on my phone. It shows him in the hotel.

Breakfast.

I bet he's in the lobby seeing if he can get a mimosa minus the orange juice. I call him after searching the lobby and the restaurant serving a breakfast buffet. The chances of him answering are nearly zero. He's great at calling me at all hours but refuses to answer when I, or anyone, calls him.

"This is Bill; I'm not answering right now. Leave a message or call Alice, Keeper of All Things." I cringe hearing his voicemail. I've asked him repeatedly to change it. My mom is no longer his "Keeper of All Things." By default, that's my job, and I'm doing a shitty job of it today.

One more time, I check the hotel room in case we missed each other on the elevators.

No luck.

Plopping onto his bed, my butt hits something. I pull back the bedding and discover his phone—silenced and alight with a missing call from me. Great. He's wandering around without his phone. I write him a note and leave it on the desk beside his phone.

CALL ME ASAP!

Before I reach the door, I get a text.

"Fuck ..."

Anna: At least I get to wake up to one of the Steinmann men

Anna: Just not the one I expected

Eric: I'm so sorry

Eric: Please don't engage with him

Eric: Don't give him any alcohol

Eric: He'll fall asleep soon. On my way!

Anna: LOL He's lovely. Take ur time

Anna: Make sure u bring us breakfast <3

Lovely? No. My dad is not lovely. He's slippery and draining. He's a walking advertisement for depression and a host of other mental issues. Lovely ... he is not.

Against my better judgment, I stop for bagels before going to Anna's. I waste no time getting inside the house and kicking off my shoes.

"Morning, son." Dad greets me with a sly grin before sipping something from a coffee mug.

Please let it be actual coffee.

Anna sips something from a mug as well. When my gaze slides to hers, she smiles, and her cheeks turn pink. Making a quick glance at her leg, I feel a little bad for my impatience last night. I feel ... ten percent guilty. Who am I kidding? It's closer to five percent.

"What, uh..." I return my attention to my dad "...

are you doing here? And how did you get here?" I ask through gritted teeth.

"Cab. And I was afraid you were having all the fun without me."

Perfect. Why do I get the impression that his idea of "fun" is something he saw on a porn site?

Clearing my throat, I set the bagels on the counter and retrieve plates and a knife for the cream cheese. "How did you get here without an address?" I do my best to control my frustration, but it's hard. It had to be creepy as fuck for Anna when my father, whom she had never met before today, just showed up unannounced.

"I paid attention to your location last night and managed to find the right house on the third try."

Handing Anna and my dad their bagels, I offer a smile as stiff as my tightly wound nerves. "How Sherlock Holmes of you."

"I thought so," he says with pride.

Anna giggles while I pour myself a cup of coffee and sit beside my dad. "Will asked me about my thoughts on helping him get your mom back."

I cough on my coffee, banging my fist on my chest while eyeing him through narrowed eyes. "W-Will?" I cough some more. Does she know my dad's name is William? He's gone by Bill forever. Will is a young kid, a moderately put-together architect living in the burbs, not a sixty-year-old man who hasn't had his toenails clipped in so long he could climb a tree with them.

"Anna came up with it," he winks at her.

What the fuck? He's winking at my girl? Okay, she's not mine. Not yet, but I'm working on it, and I don't need a sidekick.

"Is that so?" I scratch the back of my head, eyeing Anna.

She shrugs, dusting the cinnamon and sugar from her fingers. "He introduced himself as William, and it felt too formal. I asked if anyone called him 'Will,' and he said only the pretty girls."

Unbelievable.

"Well, *Will*, seeing you in such a good mood is nice. And showered. That's a bonus."

"Anna loaned me her loofah." Again, he winks at her.

I no longer care about his winks. *He showered here?!*

Anna curls her lips between her teeth and gives me another shrug—enough with the shrugs and winks. I don't find any of this funny, flirty, or worthy of shrugging off.

"Why, exactly, would you shower here instead of at the hotel?"

"No loofah." Dad takes a big bite of his bagel, cream cheese oozing past the corners of his mouth onto his closely shaven face. Did he use her razor too?

It doesn't matter.

The more significant issue is the loofah. When he was forced to move out of his house, he stole my mom's favorite loofah. She got it in India. Dad uses it to exfoliate his crack on the rare occasions he showers.

"I'm so sorry," I murmur to Anna.

"What? No. Don't be sorry. I'm glad he's here. I just hope you weren't too worried about him. He said he accidentally left his phone in the hotel room."

I'm not sure there's much my father does by accident. He was the most intelligent, put-together man I knew ... until he wasn't. My mom is a witch. That's the only explanation that makes sense. She put a curse on him that drained every ounce of his dignity. Maybe it's not just my mom. Maybe that's the curse of all women. Eyeing Anna for a second, I give that more thought.

Admittedly, I'm impulsive around her. When we're together, I willingly do anything to touch her, see her growing smile, and hear her addictive laughter. It's fucking witchcraft.

"Worried ..." I twist my lips, staring at my coffee. "I'm not sure that's the right word."

"Controlling," Dad says. "Eric likes to tell me what to do, when to do it, and how to do it. I don't know who he thinks raised him."

"Mom raised me." I mock him with the same ridiculous kind of wink he gave Anna.

"That's because you suckled at the teat until you went to school. What do they call that..." he snaps his fingers several times. "Cockblocking. You were a little cockblocker."

Anna snorts.

Dad reaches over and squeezes my shoulder. "But I forgive you."

"I didn't 'suckle at the teat' until I went to school.

Your memory sucks." I can't say the words and keep a straight face. After the initial embarrassment wears off, I find great pleasure in seeing my dad like this.

Smiling.

Laughing.

Joking.

Showered.

Eating.

Drinking something besides alcohol.

Alive. My dad's taken an enormous step away from the drain.

I'm too damn happy about that to care about the circumstances that brought it to fruition—namely, Anna. She makes everything better. Don't get me wrong; I will have to burn the loofah and thoroughly clean her bathroom. Ten bucks says his streaked underwear is sitting on her vanity next to the sink.

"Nah ..." Dad sits back, resting his arm along the back of the sofa. "Eric was a good baby. Never cried. Slept through the night. Walked at nine months. His first word was bye-bye because She ..." He clears his throat and gives Anna a half smile. "*Alice* used to say, 'Tell your daddy bye-bye.' And she took his chubby little wrist and made him wave to me before I headed to work. And reading ... Eric was reading chapter books by four—such a smart little peanut. And, of course, his mother and I loved it since our family owned a publishing company. Did he mention that, Anna?"

I'd rather go back to talking about me suckling at my mom's teat than discuss books and publishing. And

... my dad's lying about all of it. Is this his idea of being a wingman? I was the opposite of everything he just said.

Anna doesn't skip a beat. "He did mention that." She sips her coffee, not giving me a single glance.

"Are you an avid reader?" he asks.

I try to sink into the sofa, hoping the oversized cushions swallow me whole.

"I love books. We had a book club when I lived in Des Moines in the same complex as Eric. Eric joined us shortly after he moved into the building. Did he mention that to you?"

Fuck. Make it stop. I didn't tell my family about Anna. But I was honest about her book. I said it wasn't the right fit for our publishing house, and coffee got spilled on my copy of it, so I had nothing to send back to them with notes.

"You were in a book club?" Dad's head tips back on a hearty laugh. "That must have been interesting."

"I was—" I start to defend myself, but Anna cuts me off.

"Why do you say that, Will?"

Will. Can she stop calling him that?

"Eric has a very selective taste in books. Don't get me wrong; his taste is impeccable, but not many books make it onto his short list of recommendations. I imagine him being a Scrooge in a book club."

Scrubbing my hands over my face, I grumble nothing in particular, just displeasure and pain. "Dad, we should let Anna rest. She's still recovering from her injury."

"Eric didn't like the book our club read," Anna says, taking a roller truck to my heart and squeezing every last bit of regret from it.

I keep my head bowed in shame. What can I say?

"Did everyone else like it?" Dad asks.

"Yes. But there was no requirement to like the book. However, there was this one girl who *loved* the book. I mean ... you would have thought she wrote the book. And she was not a fan of Eric's critique."

Dad chuckles.

"I was a dick." My gaze stretches from the mug of coffee to Anna's innocent eyes.

What's her crime? Being passionate about telling a story?

"I think she was caught up in the story and missed the finer details, like how the story could have been told better. It could have been more concise, better edited, and less indulgent in areas," Anna says.

"Sounds like you know your stuff," Dad says to Anna. "No wonder Eric's so smitten with you."

Anna blushes, and maybe I do too. But I don't look away, even when she averts her gaze. I'm smitten as fuck with her. And I'm owning it. Maybe I have no idea where we're going. Maybe we have nowhere to go. It's pretty much the theme of my life. Why should my love life be any different?

Love.

Do I love Anna?

"What do you think? Should we head back to the hotel and let her rest?" Dad stands, taking his mug and plate to the kitchen.

"Stay," Anna says to him while returning her gaze to me. "I need to shower, but I'd love for you both to stay if you don't have other plans."

"Thanks for the offer, Anna. But I nap at one, and I have a feeling Eric wants you to himself for a while."

I lift a shoulder. He's not wrong.

Anna bites her lip to hide her grin.

"Mind getting me a cab?" Dad asks.

I hold out the key fob to the rental car. "Think you can find your way back to the hotel?"

He snatches the key. "Who do you think taught you everything you know about navigation?"

"Mom," I say.

"No respect." He shakes his head while squeezing Anna's arm. "It's been a pleasure, young lady."

"When are you going home? We should have dinner tonight."

Dad releases her arm. "When you get back on both feet, come visit, and I'll take you to my favorite place in Kansas City. A friend of mine owns a bistro. They're booked out for months, but he'll squeeze us in. How does that sound?"

"I'm not sure when I'll be mobile enough to travel, but I'll put that trip on my wish list."

"Fair enough."

"Bye, Dad." I'm stunned. Never did I imagine the

events that happened this morning. "Do you have your key to the room?"

"Of course," he says on the way to the front door as if he'd never forget it, even though he forgot his phone. "Call me when you need me to get you."

"I will. Did you forget your bag upstairs? Do you have your underwear on Anna's vanity?"

Dad says nothing, but he pivots and heads up the stairs.

Anna laughs while I take her plate and mug to the kitchen with mine.

A few minutes later, Dad gives us a silent wave before the door clicks shut behind him.

"I don't know what to say." I stand next to her chair and slide my hands into my pockets. "I never thought he'd show up unannounced."

"I never thought you'd leave me without a note or something to confirm that last night happened."

"Oh," I take the weight of her injured leg in one hand while my other hand lowers the recliner, "last night happened. But if you don't remember, I could remind you." Kneeling in front of her, I lean forward, resting my hands on her thighs, stopping just before our lips meet. "Thank you for being so kind and gracious with my dad," I whisper.

Anna presses her palms to my face for a breath before running her fingers through my hair. I nearly shiver. "Your dad asked me if I thought he should go after your mom to get her back."

"Oh?"

Anna's gaze slides along my face, and I feel it as much as her physical touch. "I told him to let her go. If they're meant to be together, it will happen. He has to trust the universe."

"Do you trust the universe?"

Her smile fades. I feel that too. "Eric, I'm ..."

"You're what?"

"I love my job here. And there's a chance I could get transferred to their firm in Barcelona."

"Spain?" I put a few more inches of space between us.

Her hands leave my hair, flopping onto the chair's arms. "Yes. There's a chance. A small one, but I'm hopeful, or at least I was hopeful until the accident ... until—"

"No." I sit back on my heels. "Not *until* anything. You should go for it. If you get this chance and don't take it, you'll always regret it."

Indecision takes up residency on her face.

I stand on my knees again and take her beautiful face in my hands. "It's okay that last night happened, *and* it's okay for you to go to Spain." My lips press to hers for a long kiss before my mouth makes its way along her jaw to her ear. "It's also okay to do it again right now. We don't have to be more than this moment."

"Eric ..."

"I love all our little moments." I kiss her neck and lift the hem of her T-shirt.

"I ... I need to shower." She teases the nape of my neck with her fingers.

I pull her shirt over her head and grin, removing my shirt in the next breath. Those lines of indecision still mar her face, but they don't stop her hands from working the button and zipper of my jeans.

Grabbing her ass, I pull her to the edge of the recliner so that her nipples brush my chest. I feel her lips pull into a grin along my shoulder. "Know what I love?" she whispers.

"What's that, baby?" My hands slide into the back of her panties.

"I love the feeling of you inside of me."

I smile, quite possibly more prominent than I've ever smiled before. "Yeah?"

She nods, sucking the skin along my neck while releasing me from my briefs. My breath catches in my throat. I have no direction in my life because this woman is the sunrise for which I wait in the dark to chase after every long night. The past three years have been the longest fucking night of my life. And I don't want to live without her, but I won't ever stand in the way of her dreams again.

"I also love..." her breaths fall heavily on my skin as I slide the crotch of her panties aside "...when you call me *baby*." Her head falls back, eyes closed, when I push inside her.

I love *her*.

CHAPTER
TWENTY-THREE

Anna

It's been nice visiting my heart. Eric effortlessly took it three years ago. Even if he crushed it in his hand, he never let go. He idly waits for me to walk away. And he's doing it again.

But I'm not leaving today.

Not after making love in the living room.

Not after taking a bath together in Shaun's soaker tub.

And probably not after this trip to the grocery store.

"This is why I get grocery delivery." I huff, blowing my hair out of my face while Eric deposits groceries into the basket of the motorized shopping cart. I can't believe he talked me into this. There's probably a little old lady being forced to push a big cart around the store because Eric insisted we make a trip to the store, followed by his refusal to let me navigate the store on my crutches.

"I'm so turned on right now," he says while reading the label of the salsa verde. "You handle that scooter like a boss."

"Stop," I giggle, shaking my head.

"I'm banking at least fifty different wet dreams."

"Eric ... stop!" I speed ahead of him before someone hears him and associates him with me. I live around here, but he can be obnoxious without embarrassing future repercussions.

"Anna Banana, are you pretending we're not together?" He hollers so anyone within a three-aisle radius can hear him.

It reminds me of when he called me out to our neighbor after I screamed, "Eric Fucking Steinmann," during an orgasm in his apartment.

"I've threatened to tie you to the bed but never followed through. Today feels like that day. Don't you agree?"

Jesus. I hate him almost as much as I love him. *Almost.*

I snag items from the shelves without completely stopping and toss them into the basket.

"Anna ..." He's catching up, so I speed up.

When I make a quick right, there's a grunt, a crash, and a shatter.

"Oh my god! I'm so sorry." I try to stand, but Eric grabs my shoulders, guiding me back to the scooter seat.

"There's glass, Anna. Just stay put," he says.

Several bystanders and an employee converge on the scene of the accident. A woman, probably in her fifties, hugs her elbow and winces from the pool of pickles, pickle juice, and glass on the floor.

"You have *no* business being on that," she seethes, scowling at me while Eric helps her up with her good arm. "I bet that's a fake boot. You're pathetic."

"She's not. Just reckless," Eric murmurs. "Is your arm okay?"

"I don't know. It hurts, and YUCK! I smell like pickles. This is a brand-new shirt."

Biting my lips together, I fight something between tears and laughter. It's almost an out-of-body experience. Did I really just mow down a lady and her jar of pickles with the store's motorized shopping cart?

Eric Steinmann continues to bring out the worst in me. Once a drug. Always a drug.

The lady moves her arm back and forth a few times.

"Probably just a bruise," Eric says, digging his wallet out of his front pocket. "Will five hundred cover the blouse?" He holds up a wad of cash.

She stares at it, then at him, and smiles with a tiny nod. When her gaze shifts to me, her resting bitch face returns.

"I'm so sorry," I whisper.

Eric puts his hand over mine on the handle and reverses the cart. "We have enough groceries for today. Let's go check out."

"No. Let's leave it and go home."

"What? No. It was an accident. All is good."

No. It's not good. And here I thought his embarrassingly suggestive comments would ruin it for me to ever return to this store. I never imagined it would be a hit-and-run.

Okay, I didn't run, but only because my crutches were in the back of my car, and I couldn't run.

On the way home, I keep my sunglasses on, and my head turned toward the window, but I feel Eric's occasional glance in my direction. I know he's grinning.

My phone vibrates.

Shaun: I'll be home tomorrow. You doing okay?

Anna: I'm good. How's ur mom?

Shaun: She seems to have rebounded

Shaun: My sister's here, so I'm coming home for a few days to take care of some business

Shaun: I'll be back here next week or sooner if anything changes

Anna: Safe travels

Shaun: Thx

"Everything okay?" Eric asks.

"It's Shaun. He's coming home tomorrow. His

mom is doing a little better, so he's going to take care of some things before going back there next week."

"That's good."

"Yeah," I murmur.

We pull into the driveway, and Eric jumps out like it's a fire drill, bringing me my crutches before I can open my door.

"My lady," he says, opening the door.

I roll my eyes. "Chivalry won't work this time."

"No? Why not?"

"Because I nearly killed someone at the grocery store, and it was all your fault." I climb out and tuck the crutches under my arms.

Eric wraps his arms around me and kisses me hard. I lose my balance, so he hugs me tighter and kisses me harder while my crutches fall.

I turn my head for a breath of air. "You never play fairly."

"Play fairly?" He ensures I'm stable on one leg before he bends down to retrieve my crutches. "I'm not playing anything. I just wanted to kiss you because you're irresistible when you pretend to be mad at me."

"I'm not pretending."

"Baby ..." he draws out the word, angering me that I find it sexy. But I do. "You kissed me back with a good amount of tongue and a soft moan. If that's your idea of being mad, I might work harder to keep you mad."

"I see you're still arrogant."

He chuckles, opening the back hatch to get the bags of groceries. "And you're still mistaking my confidence for arrogance." He closes the door and twists his lips. "It's not even confidence. More like bold hope."

I follow him to the door. "Bold hope?"

"Yes. I always *hope* you want me to kiss you, and I've managed to be bold enough with my efforts that it's easily mistaken for confidence or, your word, arrogance." He holds open the door while I hobble into the house. "But there's always a little doubt in my mind because I know you're not a sure thing."

Eric takes the bags to the kitchen. "But I'm pretty damn elated when I get to be with you and when you kiss me back. Best feeling in the world."

Never ever, *ever* has he played fairly. Eric knows my biggest weakness, and he plays on my weakness. He makes me question my feelings, my decisions, and my entire life.

"I'm going to look for a flight back to Kansas City. Hopefully, something early in the morning. And tonight, I can clean the house so it's in tip-top shape when Shaun gets home tomorrow. After I put away the groceries, I'll mow the lawn if there's gas for his mower. He shouldn't have to mess with any of that if he's only coming home for a short time."

"It's an electric mower. And you don't have to mow the lawn."

"I know, but I want to," Eric says, glancing over his shoulder while he unpacks the groceries.

He's a good man, and that truth messes with my thoughts as common sense and raw emotion clash in a battle of wills.

ERIC DOES everything he promised while I sit helplessly in my chair and try to focus on my next work project, but it's hard because he's leaving. And I don't know what comes next, what everything means, or if it means anything. We're "moments." But when will we have more moments? In three weeks? Three months? Three more years? I feel utterly inept with words.

Fucking up words is supposed to be Eric's thing. Not mine.

"Your dad's here," I say when I see him on the front door camera the following morning.

Eric's been hellbent on making sure the kitchen is spotless from breakfast. "Tell Shaun I'm thinking of him, and I hope his mom continues to get better," he says, lifting his bag onto his shoulder.

"I will." I stand by the front door with my heart in my throat.

"I'll call you," he says, framing my face.

Finding my bravest smile, I hold my breath. It feels like the slightest misstep could send my emotions into a tailspin.

"My dad was serious about you coming to Kansas for a visit and dinner."

I nod several times.

"You're going to be out of that boot and running laps in no time."

"Hope so," I manage to say with some control.

"When will you know about Spain?"

Spain. Why did I tell him about that?

"I have no idea. Could be in a few weeks or a few months. Since my accident, my boss has been pretty vague about it. I fear she's working up the nerve to tell me I didn't get the promotion. She just doesn't want to tell me until I'm literally back on my feet."

He kisses me, and I feel the emotions all the way to my toes. I've done it again. I've let him consume me. "Or ..." He brushes his nose against mine. "Your boss is waiting until you're fully recovered so she can give Spain a start date. Stay positive. Okay?"

Positive?

I'm in love with him, and he's calling the possibility of an ocean separating us "positive?" I can barely handle the 554.6 (yes, I googled it) miles between us. An ocean? I can't imagine.

"Positive. Got it."

Again, he kisses me. This time tears burn my eyes, threatening to expose all of my emotions. I moan into the kiss, encouraging him to keep kissing me, buying myself a little time to shore up the dam.

"Bye, baby," he whispers while running his thumb along my lip.

"Bye."

CHAPTER TWENTY-FOUR

Eric

"Do you want to talk about it?" My dad unbuckles his seat belt the second we reach cruising altitude.

"About what?" I stare out the window at the nearly cloudless sky.

"The girl. Anna."

"What do you want to know about her?"

"I mean, do you want to talk about ... you know. Your feelings and shit."

With a dry chuckle, I shake my head. "I think I'm good. When did you get into talking about 'feelings and shit'? Because for many months, I've been at your disposal, ready and moderately willing to listen to your *feelings and shit* about—"

"Her."

I turn toward him. "You said Mom's name to Anna, so I know you can say it."

"I was trying to be on my best behavior for you."

"Yeah, about that. Where has this best behavior been? I thought you lost the best of yourself with your house in the divorce."

He twists his lips and drums his gray-haired fingers on his thighs. "Anna reminds me of Her. When your mom was young, She had passion." Dad clears his throat. "Well, a different kind of passion than the missing one for which She supposedly left me. I don't think I could share Her in bed with someone else."

"Dad," I rub my forehead, "I don't think Mom's looking for *that*."

"She loved the explicit novels. What did Mike use to call it? Mommy porn?"

"Yeah, I don't think the adult romance community warmly accepts that term."

He waves his hand in the air. "You know what I'm talking about. Lots of nipples, clits, and cocks. Moaning. Multiple orgasms. That shit's ruining marriages. Setting the bar impossibly high for men."

I think of the time I reenacted the sex scene from Anna's book. She was all in. I didn't feel like the bar was set too high. I felt like she gave me a ladder and a clear map of how to reach said bar.

"Maybe you should read some of those books. They're much different from those videos you watch on your computer."

He grumbles. "You know, after getting out of the shower, she asked me to talk dirty to her—"

"Dad, no. Please. I don't need to—"

"I told her to bend over and clean the toilet. I slept on the sofa that night."

"Let's talk about Anna. I'll share my feelings. Just ..." I pinch the bridge of my nose. "Please don't share your sex life with me."

"Sex life? We didn't have sex that night. And she didn't even clean the toilet."

"Shh ..." I scoot down in my chair when I feel other passengers staring at us. We're done talking.

I TEXT Anna when we get home.

> Eric: Home

> Eric: Is Shaun there?

Anna: Glad to hear u had a safe trip

Anna: His plane just landed. He should be here in 30

> Eric: I'll be here catching up on work. Call or FaceTime if ur bored

Anna: Same to u <3

I grin and call her.
She answers with a giggle. "Bored already?"
"My responsibilities are boring."
"I'm boring."
"No." I close my bedroom door when my dad walks past my room to his bathroom. Putting her on

speaker, I toss the phone on my bed to unpack my bag. "You are anything but boring."

She sighs. "Is it too soon to miss you?"

My chest swells, and I want to pound my fists against it. "I can jump on a plane and visit anytime. Just say the word."

"Jump on a plane and come visit me."

I laugh, tossing my dirty clothes into the hamper. "I'm sure Shaun could use a friend. You make everything better. Do your magic. I'll be knocking at your door again before you know it."

"Pfft. I don't think I can make his situation better."

"His situation is one of pain. He's in pain. You're the perfect salve." As I say the words, I internally cringe. Shaun looks at her like I've looked at her. And I'd be lying if I said that doesn't fuck with my head.

"Eric ..."

"Anna." I move my phone to the bathroom vanity while unpacking my toiletries.

"It's easier to deal with you so far away when you say the wrong word. Say something stupid. Insult my favorite book or my taste in art. Make me feel better about the distance between us. Just stop saying the right thing. I don't know what to do with that—not from you."

I laugh, sitting on the tub's edge and running my hands through my hair. I fucking love this woman. And maybe I should say it. Just ... throw it out there. Would it be the right word? Or would it, once again, derail her life when she's so hopeful about this job in Spain?

"Since you asked, I have to say ... the color of your car is a little—"

"A little what?"

"Old lady."

"Old lady?"

"Yes. It's light brown metallic with a beige interior."

"I got a good deal on it. Nearly half the price of other cars with low miles."

"You got a good deal on it because everyone else interested in that color no longer has a driver's license —or a pulse, for that matter."

She gasps, and I can picture her jaw hanging low, eyes squinted, and shoulders hugging her ears. "Eric Steinmann, that's just—"

"I love you, Anna."

Shit. I wasn't going to say it. Not yet.

But every time I exhale, I feel those words leave my chest in a tiny whisper. The only way I can breathe is by letting them out.

She says nothing.

"I'm sorry." I squeeze my eyes shut. "I mean, I'm not sorry that I love you. I'm sorry if hearing those words imparts any sort of responsibility. It's not a plea or a question. I expect nothing in return. It changes nothing. Okay? Dream big. Be a million times more responsible and successful than me. I mean ... you already are."

"Eric—"

"I think it's my dad struggling to deal with my

mom. And Shaun dealing with his sick mom. It's got me thinking about life's fragility and our bonds with people."

"Eric—"

"Giving and receiving love is important. It doesn't even have to be in a romantic way. You know? It's a confidence builder. Or it should be. You can be a little more awesome because you have *so* many people who love you." I pick up my phone and head back to my bedroom, pacing like an addict.

"Eric—"

"I'm not saying how I feel about you isn't romantic. It is, but the love isn't needy. It's like the kind of love you can take or leave. If you need it, great. If not, no big deal. Think of it as complementary shampoo and soap at a hotel."

I'm a *fucking idiot!*

That was the worst declaration of love ever. I mean, EVER.

"Hey, Shaun. I'll be off the phone in just a sec," Anna says.

"I'll let you go, Anna. Good talk. Say 'hi' to Shaun."

I press end.

"Fuck ..." I cock my arm back, readying to heave my phone against the wall. Then on a slow exhale, I deflate and gather my composure.

CHAPTER TWENTY-FIVE

Anna

I KEEP my head bowed away from Shaun while I pull it together. Eric loves me—a word-fumbling, palpably nervous kind of love. And that put a big smile on my face, but when I got a glance at Shaun, he looked drained in every way possible. So now I must clear my throat and ditch the smile before lifting my head.

He plops down onto the sofa with a hard sigh. Long lines run across his forehead and spread out from the corners of his weary eyes.

"So your mom's doing better. That's good."

His empty gaze locks onto the marble coasters stacked on the coffee table. After several slow blinks, he shakes his head. "She's not," he whispers.

"I thought you said—"

"I lied."

"Why would you lie?"

His gaze inches its way to mine. "I wanted it to be true. So I put it into the world and prayed it would become a reality."

"Then why are you here? If she's not getting better ..."

Shaun's eyes redden. "I couldn't watch her ... die," he whispers, choking on his last word.

His confession twists my heart into a knot, obliterating the joy I felt on the phone with Eric just minutes earlier. "Shaun." I lower my chair and hop to the sofa next to him.

The muscles in his jaw clench while he shakes his head. He doesn't want to cry in front of me. I don't let it stop me from wrapping my arms around him in a big hug. Shaun's been there for me at every turn. He's seen me at my physical and emotional worst.

After a second of hesitation, he slides his arms around my waist, hugging me tightly while his body shakes. I don't let go. Sometimes you don't know what you need until someone shows you—forces you to share the burden. I can't stop what's happening to his mom, but maybe I can take some of the emotional burden. And maybe it will be enough for him to go back and be with her when she takes her last breath.

And if not, that's okay too. Death isn't a test or a lesson of anything. It's the worst part of life. Period.

"Anna ... I needed this."

I hug him tighter.

"I needed you," he whispers.

I smile.

He turns his head a fraction, pressing a kiss to my cheek.

I think of my life's path. And for a split second, it crosses my mind that it wasn't meant to be my time with Eric when I lived in Des Moines. Maybe my path brought me here to help Shaun at this very moment.

That split second ends when he kisses my cheek again, letting his lips linger. And again, he kisses my cheek, but this time it's closer to the corner of my mouth. I stop breathing despite my racing heart. Everything in my head turns to mush like the day Eric confessed he knew I wrote *The Last Person*.

I feel exposed and lost. It's the worst kind of fragility. I want to cry and hide from the world. Guilt washes over me. Did I do this? Is this my fault?

"Anna." It's a plea like he's asking for permission or validation.

I stiffen, releasing him, but I can't look him in the eye. "I, uh ... need to shower. I have a huge project to finish. And I need to, uh..." I scramble, reaching for my crutches "...nail this for the best chance of getting that job in Spain."

"Anna?"

I make it to standing in record time, distancing myself from Shaun. When I can't help but look at him, he gives me a sad smile, shoulders slumped.

"I didn't mean to make you—"

"You didn't make me anything. I'm so sorry about your mom. You have to feel out of sorts right now. I know that feeling all too well. I'm kinda still struggling with my life too. If you want to talk, I'm here. But I think you know the right thing to do is go back and be with your mom and your sister."

And never kiss me like that again.

Resting his elbows on his knees, Shaun bows his head. "I'm sorry, Anna."

"Nothing to apologize for." I make my way to the stairs. "We're good. It's all ... good."

It's not.

It's as far from good as things can be. I can't stay here.

LATER THAT NIGHT, Shaun knocks on my bedroom door. "Dinner."

"Uh ... I'm not hungry, but thanks."

"Anna, open the door."

I sigh. The chances of moving out without facing him again are slim, so I open the door and hobble back to my bed, sitting on the end of it. I feel his gaze on me, but I don't want to look at him. When he doesn't say anything, I'm forced to look up.

"I'm so sorry I made you uncomfortable." He leans against the doorframe and crosses his arms.

"You weren't in your right mind. It's fine."

"You're hiding in your room; it's not fine."

I frown because anything else would be a lie, and we both know it. "It was unexpected," I murmur.

"I'm sorry it was unexpected, and I'm sorry I made you uncomfortable—"

"I said it's fine. You were—"

"Anna, let me finish."

Pressing my lips together, I give him a tiny nod.

"I'm not sorry I did it. I'm not sorry about my feelings for you. I needed to know how you felt about me, and now I do. We're good. I don't want things to be awkward."

I shake my head. "Feelings for me? What are you talking about? Earlier, you were confused, grieving the imminent loss of your mother, and you—"

"Felt vulnerable enough to do what I've wanted to do for many months."

My lips part, but words escape me. He's wanted to do this for months?

Shaun sighs. "I thought there was something there, just under the surface. Since you've been here, we've clicked. We laugh and joke with each other. We make meals together. We like the same movies. I loved that you helped me so much with the remodel. It turned out perfect. Clearly, I was wrong about us. But I had to know."

Truth?

I'd be lying if I said I'd never thought of Shaun in a romantic way, but those thoughts felt wrong and were always fleeting. Making dinner together did start to feel natural and domestic. Sometimes I'd see him by the pool with his shirt off, and I took notice. He's handsome and fit. His peppering of gray in his whiskers and sideburns only makes him sexier.

When he's had women spend the night (which hasn't been often), I've heard them, and it was impossible to keep from wondering what it would be like to be with him in that way. But ... *but* ... that's it. They were thoughts. Innocent thoughts that went no further than my mind.

"Say something, Anna."

"It's not crazy. And ... I don't know. Maybe, under different circumstances, I would have been more receptive to the idea of us being more. But ..."

"Eric is the *but*."

I nod.

"Are you two a thing now? I can't see you in a long-distance relationship. And I thought you were hoping to go to Spain."

I lift my gaze to his. "Were you ... I mean, if I had the same feelings for you now, were you going to try and talk me out of the job if it was ... *is* offered to me?"

"Of course not." His head jerks backward.

"Then why? Why go there now when you know I might be moving?"

"Jesus, Anna ..." He pushes off the side of the door-frame and runs his hands through his hair. "If you felt about me the way I feel about you, I'd pack my bags and follow you to Spain. I just want to be with you."

The wrong guy is saying the right thing. My heart sinks.

"I'm ... flattered."

"Fuck, Anna. I don't want you to be flattered. And..." he laces his fingers behind his neck "...I should have said it months ago. And maybe it would have made a difference, and maybe it wouldn't have. But it's out there now. I can't take it back, and I don't want to take it back. Just know that you owe me nothing."

I owe him *so* much.

"I think I need to move out."

"No, Anna. Don't do that. This doesn't have to change a thing. I ..." He blows out a long breath. "I have to go back to be with my mom. I shouldn't have left, and you helped me see that. But I want to talk about this more. I want things to be okay. If you get that job in Spain, great. But don't leave just because you don't feel comfortable here with me. Promise me you won't make any decisions until we talk more."

His desperation wears me down, and I nod.

"Thank you. Now, will you come downstairs and eat?"

Another nod.

CHAPTER TWENTY-SIX

Eric

"You've been avoiding me?" I say as soon as Anna answers her phone. Over the past week, she's found every excuse not to FaceTime with me or answer my calls. She's been replying to my texts, but only with a few words and emojis.

"A little."

I don't expect her honesty.

"Why?" I ask.

"Shaun lied about his mom. She's not doing better."

"I'm sorry to hear that. Did you ever meet her?"

"No."

"I take it he's having a rough time?"

"Probably. We haven't talked much since he left here to be with her again. He's staying another few days to help his sister go through their mom's belongings and get things settled at her house. They don't think she'll go back home. A care facility is the next option."

"O-kay ... so that's why you've been avoiding me?"

She doesn't respond.

"I've had a lot on my mind. Many decisions," she finally says.

"Decisions? Did you hear back about the job?"

"Not yet."

"Then what decisions?" *Fuck ... is she breaking up with me?*

"I think I need to move."

"Move? Out of Nashville?"

"Out of this house."

"Why?"

Again, there's a long pause. "It's weird, me living with Shaun. He needs his space, and I'm sure my presence isn't exactly great for his dating life."

"You didn't think it was weird when I asked about it. How did it suddenly become weird?"

"I don't know. I'm just ... ready for something different."

"Why would you consider moving before you find out if you have the job in Spain? Why risk having to move twice or signing a lease and—"

"Jesus, Eric! Why are you grilling me on this?"

I hold the phone away from my ear.

"I'm ..." she huffs. "I'm sorry. I'll talk with you later."

"Anna?"

She's already ended the call.

"Trouble in paradise?" My dad asks, poking his head in my bedroom.

I should have shut the door, but he doesn't hear anything most of the time and refuses to get hearing aids, but when something's none of his business, it's like I'm wiretapped, and he's on the opposite end of the line with perfect hearing.

"No. But thanks for eavesdropping ... I mean *checking in.*"

"She's probably upset that you flew to Nashville to get some action and left without doing something extra."

"Extra?" I walk to the door and shut off my light, forcing him to head toward the living room in front of me.

"Flowers. Jewelry. A poem."

"Are you really giving me advice on women?"

He backs into his recliner, plunking down with a grunt. "I was married for nearly forty years. I think that earns me the right to impart some wisdom onto my only child."

"A few weeks ago, you were considering a three-some because you thought that's what Mom meant when she said she needed more passion. If that's the level of wisdom you're implying, I'll pass."

"Then what do you suggest? We both pine for the women we love for the rest of our lives? Spend the rest of our miserable lives golfing and masturbating?"

"I don't golf. I had sex recently, so my need to

masturbate is not a high priority. And I have Anna. I haven't lost her like you lost Mom. So don't lump me in with you like we're going through the same experience."

"Then what's the problem?" He's good at goading me.

"I don't know if there's a problem. She's having a bad day. I'm sure it will be fine the next time we talk."

"You love her?"

I nod.

"Does she love you?"

I hesitate. She hasn't said as much, but I know she does.

Doesn't she?

"She doesn't love you?"

"I didn't say that."

"You didn't have to."

I water my plants to keep from letting him see my insecurities.

"What are your plans for this girl? She told me she's hoping to get a job in Spain. That's in Europe, buddy."

"Thanks for the geography lesson, Dad."

"If it were me—"

"It's not you."

"If you love her, then what's the problem?"

"Do you love Mom?"

He puckers his lips to the side. "Point taken. I'm just saying, don't be like me and muck it all up."

I refill the watering can. "Solid advice. Thanks."

An hour later, Anna texts me.

Anna: Sorry

Eric: Don't be

Eric: Everything okay?

Anna: No

I don't know how to reply after getting in trouble for asking too many questions.

Eric: I'm here if you need me

Anna: Thank you

That's it. No more texts, not even a text bubble that tells me she wants to say more, even if she doesn't know how to say it.

I grab my shoes and chalk bag and head to the bouldering gym. Over the next three hours, I climb every problem, work out in the weight room, and sit in the sauna. By the time I head home, I'm exhausted, but my mind is calmer.

CHAPTER TWENTY-SEVEN

Anna

I GOT the job in Spain.

A dream job in a dream location. I start next month, as long as I can physically get there and navigate well enough to work in the office.

I haven't told anyone. I'm unsure who to tell first, but when Eric's name pops up on my phone, I take it as a sign.

"Hey."

"Hey. How's it going?" he asks.

"Good. Really good ... I think."

He chuckles. "That's the least convincing *really good* I've ever heard."

"I got the job in Spain," I say and immediately hold my breath, waiting for his response.

"That's ... great. I'm ... so happy for you." He

doesn't sound happy. If I failed to convince him with my response, he failed even worse with his.

"Eric?"

"Hmm?"

"I love you."

Silence.

I clear my throat. "I just need you to know it because feeling loved is nice, even if it changes nothing."

"What if it changes everything?"

"I'm taking the job."

"As you should."

"You're not mad?"

"Is this why you've been so distant?"

"I've been distant because I'm five hundred miles away from you."

"Anna."

I sigh. "I've been distant because something happened."

"What happened?"

I hate the idea of telling him, but I hate the secret more than the risk that comes with the truth. "Before Shaun went back to be with his mom, he sort of ..."

"Sort of what?"

"Kissed me."

"Fuck." The whoosh of his frustrated sigh fills my ear. "Of course, he did."

"What's that supposed to mean? I didn't encourage it. It completely caught me off guard."

"You're so blind when it comes to him."

"You mean blindsided."

"I mean, you have tunnel vision with everything. You see the world how you want it, not how it is."

"Wow. There you go again, showering me with compliments. Thanks for that. And thanks for taking my side."

"Anna, there are no sides. I love you because you are joy and happiness personified. Why wouldn't Shaun fall in love with you for the same reasons? It's not your fault that you're so amazing, but it's not his fault either."

"Yet, I'm blind. That's what you said. You implied I'm stupid and naive, living in my own little world. Sorry, Eric. You void every nice word with something offensive."

"Baby, I'm just—"

"I don't want to be your 'baby' today."

He sighs. "Anna, what do you want me to say? What do you want me to do?"

"I want you to say and do the right thing ... but I don't want to have to tell you what that is. At least Shaun said the right thing. He didn't fumble his words. He laid it all out there. And he was willing to *do* the right thing. I didn't have to tell him anything. He just knew. And maybe *that's* true love. Maybe the only one I'm wearing blinders with is you."

The first thing I feel is satisfaction. It's hard to find my voice and even harder to get the words out when they need to be said. But I've done it. I just stood up for myself. And for ten whole seconds, it feels incredible.

At the eleventh second, I realize Eric hasn't said a single word. My pride crumbles into a pile of regret.

"Jesus ... I'm sorry. Say something," I whisper.

"I don't know what to say," he says in defeat.

"Ask me if I have feelings for Shaun. Ask me if my feelings for you are more than my feelings for him. Ask me if—"

"I already know you have feelings for Shaun. And I already know your feelings for me are beyond comparison. What I don't know is if that's enough. I don't know if you know my love for you is unwavering. My love for you isn't dependent on saying or doing the right thing. My love for you accepts imperfections. But more than anything, my love for you is honest. And if you don't trust that my love for you is greater than any spoken word, greater than a critical observation about a painting, another man's feelings toward you, or *a book* ... then it isn't enough. But if my love for you isn't enough, then no one's love will be enough. And I know this because no man will love you like I do."

I can't speak with my heart wedged in my throat and tears pouring from my burning eyes. I have never felt this loved and yet so heartbroken at the same time.

"Anna, I need to know. Did you stop writing because of me? Did you try to follow your dream after you left? It's been the elephant in the room for too long. And it's fucking killing me."

Unable to swallow past the lump in my throat, I find a tiny voice, "Don't worry about me, Eric. I followed my dream." Staring at the phone, my finger hovers over the red button. When I can manage a simple "goodbye," I press *End*.

❚❚══╱❚❚❚══╲❚❚❚

Three weeks later ...

"ANNA, ARE WE GOOD?" Shaun asks while taping the last box that will get shipped to my parents' house.

I smile, closing my suitcase. "We're good."

I wanted to be out of my boot by now, but at least I can put my full weight on it. PT has helped a lot—no more crutches. I've already found a physical therapist in Barcelona to continue my rehabilitation.

"If you don't keep in touch, I'll know you're lying."

Chuckling, I stand and set my suitcase upright. I've condensed my necessary belongings into one suitcase. I'm leaving behind everything I don't need—almost everything.

"Communication is a two-way street. I'll make an effort if you do."

"Deal." Shaun gives me a half-grin. It's adorable.

I spend more time noticing Shaun's wonderful qualities, and I do it without feeling guilty or inappropriate. Had I not given my heart to another man, I think I could have given it to Shaun. I hope someday I'll feel enough love again to share it with someone else. Right now, my chest is hollow.

"If you end up not loving Spain, you're always welcome here."

I hug Shaun. "You're such a good man," I whisper in his ear.

"Well," he releases me and glances around the bedroom, "I think you're all set."

I don't miss the redness in his eyes. Eric was right, feeling loved in any form is fantastic, and everyone deserves to feel that. I don't know how to express it adequately, but I hope Shaun knows I feel his love, and it's been exactly what I've needed since the day we reconnected. He's unknowingly helped me heal from my Eric Steinmann heartbreak—twice.

"It will take me a little longer to get through security." I gesture to my boot. "So we might as well head to the airport now. I see a body cavity search in my near future."

Shaun barks a laugh. "I hope not." He takes my suitcase and heads downstairs.

I stop at my bedroom door and take one final look at the bed where I last slept with Eric.

Eric Fucking Steinmann.

"If my love for you isn't enough, then no one's love will be enough. And I know this because no man will love you like I do."

"Anna?" Shaun calls.

I wipe the few tears that have found their way to my cheeks. "Coming."

CHAPTER TWENTY-EIGHT

Eric

A FEW WEEKS AGO, Anna sent me a string of texts on her way to the airport.

> Anna: Getting on a plane to Spain.
> This is my dream
>
> Anna: I've written three novels since
> The Last Person
>
> Anna: I write for myself. It's
> therapeutic
>
> Anna: I thought I had left pieces of my
> soul in my writing
>
> Anna: I was wrong
>
> Anna: Writing feeds my soul. It makes
> me more ... not less

Anna: I love writing too much to let anyone ruin it for me. I don't want people to critique the part of my life that feels the most personal

Anna: If it weren't u, it would have been someone else

Anna: Lots of critical reviews

Anna: I'll never stop writing. When life gets hard, I write

Anna: It's my savior

Anna: I'm glad we reconnected. I feel at peace

Anna: Loving u has been a favorite pastime of mine for longer than I have ever admitted to anyone

Anna: And I won't stop anytime soon. We were almost perfect xo

Eric: Safe travels, baby xo

That's the last I heard from her.

"I have a date," Dad says. "You should shower and eat something." He frowns at me while I adjust my position on the sofa. "What are you reading?"

I show him the book cover.

"You took my advice, huh?" He smirks.

I give him the satisfaction of a submissive nod while I turn the page of my seventh romance novel in three weeks. "Technically, it was my advice to you before it was yours."

Dad laughs, adjusting his tie. "What's that saying about hiding treasures in plain sight and no one will find them? That's those damn books. Men have been trying to figure out women since the beginning of time, and women decided to hide their secrets in the very books that make us roll our eyes at them when they read them."

I hum in agreeance, closing the book and sitting up straight. "You look fly."

Dad looks down at his zipper. "My fly is up."

"You look stylish, smart, cool."

"Oh!" His eyebrows lift. They're a little bushy, but I'm in no place to nitpick.

I've grown a full beard out of sheer laziness.

"Fly is good."

I nod. "Fly is good."

He grabs his suit jacket and his keys. "Don't wait up for me." He winks.

"Tell Mom, 'hi.'"

"Will do."

After depositing my pile of plates into the dishwasher, I opt for a shower. My dad and I have swapped places. Well, almost. I'm not crying over internet porn.

However, I'm nursing a broken heart that hurts like a son of a bitch. I've typed so many messages and composed a dozen or so emails. Hell, I've purchased handmade paper and a fucking feather pen, thinking it might win me big points if Anna loves historical romance. It didn't look like a love letter; it looked like a two-year-old's finger painting. My hands are still stained black.

I've thought about sending her daily bouquets without petals, but that's nothing new. My reading has led me to believe she thinks I should have made a trip to Nashville to beat the shit out of Shaun before carrying her off to the bedroom, ordering her to get on her knees and "take every inch" while gathering her hair in my hand and calling her my "good little girl."

Or …

I tie her to the bed (which I've suggested) and declare my intention to own "every hole." I can't read that without laughing, so I'm not confident in my ability to "alpha male" her in that way.

I do know that I can't do the "daddy" thing. Her dad's alive. I fear that could get weird.

So I'm left with the most fundamental lesson to be learned from romance novels.

I'll get to that.

First, I must trim my beard, wash off this self-pity, and get to the bouldering gym. The perfect mating dance takes practice.

CHAPTER TWENTY-NINE

Anna

I LOVE MY JOB.

I hate my life.

It's complicated.

"Do you have to leave?" I give my mom and dad my best pouty face.

Mom presses her hands to my face. "We've been here two weeks. You're settled. You have a great job. A charming apartment. And minoring in Spanish is officially paying off." She kisses my forehead. "As much as I'm going to miss seeing you every few months, I feel like everything has fallen into place for you. Enjoy it, honey. I think there's a lot of exciting things coming your way."

I sigh, forcing my lips into an agreeable smile. "I know."

"Don't get mugged or raped, and you'll be fine."

"Thanks, Dad. Wise words." I roll my eyes, and so does my mom.

"If you fall in love, I want to know before you announce your engagement. Don't keep us in the dark." Mom hikes her handbag onto her shoulder.

"Don't get knocked up either." Dad slides in with the feel-good, follow-up suggestion.

"Wow. It's like you guys don't want me to have any fun." I find a genuine smile.

"Our ride's here." Dad jerks his head toward the window.

They give me one last hug, and I hold it together. It's weird how that ocean makes a big difference. I went months without seeing them, but I knew they were always a quick flight or day's drive away from me.

My heart feels extra stretched as they walk out my door. I already feel a terrible case of homesickness getting ready to set in. It's time to immerse myself in work, force myself to get out, and spend as little time alone as possible. When I take a break to catch my breath, I think of Eric, and everything hurts.

Over the next few weeks, I move forward without so much as a glance back. Momentum is all I have; I've convinced myself it's enough.

But ... yeah, I still think of Eric and wonder if I made the biggest mistake of my life.

I DIVE into my favorite coping strategy. Opening a Word document, I start at the beginning.

To everyone who doesn't believe in global warming, suck it! That smell? It's my skin burning. I bet it resembles a hog roast. Someone, please give me a quarter turn.

Des Moines, Iowa, is not immune to summer heat. Still, ninety-seven degrees on the second day of June feels like Satan has come for Midwesterners first—surprising since everyone knows Las Vegas should be his priority.

I swipe my arm across my sweaty forehead and guide my bicycle into the entry of my apartment building in East Village—a quaint neighborhood of bars, shops, and modern-industrial apartments nestled between the capitol and downtown.

"Dear god ... yes." I stop and close my eyes, letting the cool air extinguish my skin. "Yes ... yes ... yes ..." I moan, stretching the neck of my drenched, fitted tee to wipe more sweat from my face. When I open my eyes, a new face greets me, the corner of his mouth angled to show his amusement. I shoot him a tight smile. "It's really hot outside."

The words pour onto the pages so quickly that my

fingers barely keep up with the story. Like my other stories, this isn't for an agent or a publisher. This isn't a self-publishing labor of love. This is for me. I need to tell our story. My soul needs it.

I wake early to write for two hours before work and spend every single evening writing until I fall asleep mid-sentence. Our story is beautiful and messy. It's raw and painful. It's endearing ... but not enduring. And I can't get past that. Like the essence of humanity itself, we are flawed. All of our flaws are forgivable. I feel it with every chapter, through the laughter and tears, the makeups and breakups.

It's the one unforgivable flaw that haunts me. It makes it hard to focus at work. I wake in the middle of the night in a cold sweat with an achy, pounding heart. That unforgivable flaw is why I'm writing a letter of resignation. It's why I have my only suitcase on the bed awaiting my belongings. I'm not sure why this Anna character has to learn everything the hard way. It's a miracle that Eric's love for her is steady—an unwavering force like gravity.

Today, Anna Black is making the most important decision of her life. Her dream job is not enough. But now she knows what is enough.

My face hurts from grinning at my internal monologue—my third-person point of view of my life.

Sometimes you must step back and look at your life like a narrator to see that proverbial forest through the trees.

As I read over my resignation letter for the last

time, my door buzzes. I push the speaker button. "Yes?"

"I've been sitting on the bench for the past hour, watching you through your window. And I have to say, you look pretty today."

On a shaky breath, I bite my bottom lip. Tears burn my eyes. I can't talk, so I unlock the main door and tear open my fifth-floor apartment door. I don't know if my heart will survive the eternity it's taking the elevator to ascend to my floor, but it's trying.

Ding.

The doors open.

Eric makes his way to me, wearing his most charming smile and pulling a suitcase behind him. "Groveling." He smacks his hand against his forehead. "Women like men who grovel. So I've brought my groveling A-game."

I sob when the dam breaks.

"Why the tears, baby?" His question only makes my emotions double.

Releasing his suitcase, he cradles my face in his hands. "Anna, what's wrong?"

Through sniffles and hiccups, I shake my head and smile. "It's e-enough. Y-you're enough ... we're enough."

His lips slide into a slow-growing smile, filling that empty space in my chest with so much love that I can't feel the ground beneath us. "Yes. We are." He kisses me.

My favorite characters do what only Anna and

Eric would do now; they stumble back into the apartment and find the fastest route for discarding their clothes and the nearest surface to fall into each other.

The wall works for a bit.

It's rare for Eric to have his pants past his thighs before he's deep inside of me, and today is no exception.

"Anna," he says, gripping my legs and driving into me, face buried in my neck.

"Y-yeah?" I pant.

"Why is ... there a suitcase ... on your bed?"

I grab his face and kiss him. Dear god, I've missed him.

He pauses, and I release his mouth with a grin while he waits for my response. "I was going home to let Eric Fucking Steinmann love me like no other man will ever do."

Eric wears a look of pride better than anyone. "Oh, Anna Banana..." he carries me to the bed, "...and here I came all this way just to show you my mating dance. We nearly missed each other in passing." He lays me on the bed next to the suitcase.

I shove it onto the floor without taking my gaze off him.

Eric chuckles, removing the rest of his clothes. "Spread your legs, baby," he says in a husky voice.

I nearly orgasm from those four words, but I spread my legs.

"Now touch yourself," he whispers, crawling over

me, dipping his head to trap my lower lip between his teeth.

Oh god ...

If I touch myself, I will lose it. Hell, if a mouse in the corner sneezes, I'll orgasm.

"Eric, I need you ... now."

He grins, hovering over me while I'm feeling tortured in limbo. "I guess the books are right."

I narrow my eyes. "Books?"

With a laugh, he bends his head toward my breast, teasing my nipple with his tongue. "I'll tell you later."

I want to know now, but not as much as I want him back inside me.

We've always been good at this—the physical act. But this is different. It's just us. This is intimate.

This is love.

It's trust.

It's that final piece to us. That one thing that was unforgivable about us was our inability to endure. If love isn't enduring, I'm not sure it's really love.

CHAPTER THIRTY

Eric

I'M NOT LETTING her go.

That's it.

If you focus on the central underlying theme of romances that have happily ever afters, there's one simple thing the heroine wants—for the hero never to let go.

She wants to feel pursued, irreplaceable and understood. She doesn't want to feel less than anything or anyone. She wants you to walk beside her and have her back. And some days, she might need you to catch her if she starts to fall.

And if you can love her flaws, she will make you her world.

Spoiler alert: Being her world is better than winning the fucking lottery.

Anna's out. I could stare at her face all day. Her

long hair on the pillow. Her red lips in a soft smile like she's dreaming of something really good. I hope I'm in that dream. Sliding out of her bed, I use the bathroom and grab a glass of water. When I nudge her mouse to the counter's edge, her computer screen wakes up.

She wasn't kidding. If the suitcase wasn't enough proof, the resignation letter before me seals the deal. I'm not trying to snoop, but I can't *not* notice the partially visible document behind her resignation letter. Curiosity trumps her privacy. I'm a good guy, but I'm not Jesus.

It takes a few paragraphs before I let what I'm reading register. She's writing our story.

"What's your one-word first impression?" Anna asks in a sleepy voice.

I slowly turn. She pulls my T-shirt over her naked body and dangles her legs over the edge of the bed. I don't detect an ounce of anger or even nervousness. Her calmness twists my heart.

She trusts my love for her.

I love this woman completely.

And I may never find a job that feels like my calling. But I've figured out what I want to be when I grow up. I want to be in her world in whatever capacity she'll have me.

Anna Black's__________.

"Perfect."

She grins, shaking her head. "Liar."

"You know me." I sit beside her and pull her onto

my lap so she's straddling me, and her arms encircle my neck. "I'm incapable of lying about a book."

Her face softens, but her grin still holds a hint of uncertainty.

I kiss from her neck to her jaw. "Baby, our story is perfect."

She slides a hand through my hair, and it's the best feeling in the world. I live for her touch, the way I live for every smile, and those most fantastic moments when she laughs.

Anna nods. "It's *almost* perfect ... just like you."

"You could be a published author."

"I know. But I also know it's okay not to pursue that dream. It's okay to love something and not be the best at it. It's not failure. *You* helped me see that."

"Anna—"

"Kiss me." She grins. "Call me your baby." She kisses my neck. "And tell me I'm pretty. It's all I need."

EPILOGUE

The morning after Eric arrived in Spain, I messaged my mom.

> Anna: I'm in love

> Anna: Not pregnant

> Anna: No STDs

> Anna: But if he asks me to marry him, I'm saying yes

> Anna: Plan accordingly

> Mom: Is this a joke?

> Anna: No joke

I deleted my resignation letter.

Eric found us a modest house with a breathtaking view of the Mediterranean.

He's continued his freelance writing for online publications, working from home. And I've been climbing the ladder at the PR firm.

In the evenings, we polish our story.

"I don't know why you're obsessing over this," I say to him, wedging myself between him and the desk to see where he's at with the story.

He kisses my shoulder before resting his chin on it. "Yes, you do."

"I'm not publishing it," I remind him for the millionth time.

"It's such a great story."

I roll my eyes. He's been saying that for months while calling it our labor of love. Eric added chapters from his point of view and tweaked the dialogue where he thought I "misrepresented" him.

Again, it doesn't matter because no one besides us will ever read it.

"The ending, Anna. There's not really an ending."

I scroll to the last page. "We're not over. How can there be an ending?"

"Readers will want a happily ever after."

"What readers?" I laugh, twisting my neck to glance back at him.

He hasn't shaved in nearly a week. He's at his sexiest with his scruffy face, hair a tad longer around his ears, faded navy tee, and jeans. His hands hike up the skirt of my dress so he can rest them on my bare legs. Eric's obsessed with having a part of his body touching mine as much as possible. He says I ground him like I say my feet buried in the sand on the beach grounds me.

"Maybe Eric buys Anna a dog."

I giggle. Nothing makes me happier than when we talk about our story and use our own names like we didn't live it. "You think Eric buying Anna a dog is a good ending? Must be quite the dog."

"We need to nail the ending. The story's too good to botch it up with something lackluster."

"I don't think there's anything lackluster about us." I rest my hands on his when he squeezes my legs.

"Of course, you don't. But readers need more," he says.

"*We* are the only readers. This story won't end until we're dead."

"Baby, we can't die at the end. Romance readers are too fickle. They need their HEA."

Since Eric binge-read a slew of romance novels to win me over, he's acted like the foremost expert on the topic.

"Fine." I sigh. It's not worth the fight. I know this book will never leave our hands. "In the book, you can say we publish said book. Our imaginary readers will love it. But let's be honest. Readers have a weak spot for a sappy proposal and an epilogue filled with babies. So maybe you should throw that in there."

"Ya think?" he says.

"I know. They like the whole shebang."

"Then let's do it. Let's get married and have babies. I like that ending the best. I've been patiently waiting for you to suggest it."

"Whatever." I giggle, elbowing him. "If you want to write that ending, go for it."

"So that's a yes?" he asks.

"Sure."

"Anna. I need more than a sure. Is that a yes or no?"

"It's just a book."

He gasps. "Just. A. Book? Don't let my girlfriend hear you say those words. She thinks books are life. Books have souls."

"Stop throwing my words back at me. If you want an official ending, just make something up."

"It's not fiction, Anna. I can't make it up. It has to be our real life."

"It's a great ending. You flying to Spain and showing up at my door the same day I was typing my resignation letter and getting ready to pack my suitcase. It doesn't get any better than that."

Eric slides open the desk drawer to our right and fishes something out of the back. "What if it does get better?" He sets a ring box on the desk in front of me.

Everything inside of me tingles with emotion.

"What about the whole shebang?" he whispers in my ear, opening the box.

It's a rectangular emerald ring.

He removes it from the box and angles it so I see

the inside of the band and the inscription. "This is the ring my grandfather gave my grandmother when she published her first poem. My mom thought I should give it to my wife someday."

Once upon a time ...

"Anna, let's end the book with the beginning of our forever."

"Eric ..." I scoot to the side to see his face.

"Will you do me the honor of being Mrs. Eric Fucking Steinmann?" Of course, he proposes in a way that makes me laugh. I think it's his only goal in life.

Do I want to spend the rest of my life with a man who's made my happiness his full-time job and his favorite hobby all wrapped into one?

I bite my lips together. "Hmm ... this is so un-Eric of you."

He squints for a second before realization alights his face. In one swift move, he lifts me to my feet and drops to one knee, honoring his chivalrous reputation. "What's your one-word impression of my proposal?" Eric slides the ring onto my finger and glances up with a knowing grin.

"Predictable."

"Anna," he frowns.

"Sophomoric?"

He shakes his head, rejecting my word.

"Yes," I whisper.

Eric gets the girl. Anna gets a lifetime of mating dances. On their wedding day, he gives her the only copy of their love story. It's a beautiful clothbound book titled *Almost Perfect*.

Dedication

To my beautiful wife,
you look pretty today

THE END

ACKNOWLEDGMENTS

Big thanks to Jenn for nudging me to take this short story and give it more depth.

Thank you, Emily Wittig, for the perfect cover.

Monique, you are the best! Thank you for confidently jumping into the role of my editor with short notice. Thanks to the rest of my awesome editing team: Leslie, Sarah, and Bethany.

Georgana, Kim, Sarah, Christine, and the rest of the hardworking team at Valentine PR, thank you for getting my words into the hands of such gracious readers and influencers.

To my readers, I simply adore you for taking this journey with me. You've made my life a dream that I never imagined would be possible.

ALSO BY
JEWEL E. ANN

Standalone Novels

Idle Bloom

Undeniably You

Naked Love

Only Trick

Perfectly Adequate

Look The Part

When Life Happened

A Place Without You

Jersey Six

Scarlet Stone

Not What I Expected

For Lucy

What Lovers Do

Before Us

If This Is Love

Right Guy, Wrong Word

The Fisherman Series

The Naked Fisherman

The Lost Fisherman

Jack & Jill Series

End of Day

Middle of Knight

Dawn of Forever

One (*standalone*)

Out of Love (*standalone*)

Holding You Series

Holding You

Releasing Me

Transcend Series

Transcend

Epoch

Fortuity (*standalone*)

The Life Series

The Life That Mattered

The Life You Stole

Pieces of a Life

Memories of a Life

ABOUT THE AUTHOR

Jewel is a free-spirited romance junkie with a quirky sense of humor.

With 10 years of flossing lectures under her belt, she took early retirement from her dental hygiene career to stay home with her three awesome boys and manage the family business.

After her best friend of nearly 30 years suggested a few books from the Contemporary Romance genre, Jewel was hooked. Devouring two and three books a week but still craving more, she decided to practice sustainable reading, AKA writing.

When she's not donning her cape and saving the planet one tree at a time, she enjoys yoga with friends, good food with family, rock climbing with her kids, watching How I Met Your Mother reruns, and of course...heart-wrenching, tear-jerking, panty-scorching novels.

www.jeweleann.com